Angus,

thongs
and
full-
frontal
snogging

**You'll laugh
your knickers off!**

Further Confessions of Georgia Nicolson:

Angus, thongs and full-frontal snogging

'It's OK, I'm wearing really big knickers!'

'Knocked out by my nunga-nungas.'

'Dancing in my nuddy-pants!'

'...and that's when it fell off in my hand.'

'...then he ate my boy entrancers.'

'...startled by his furry shorts!'

'Luuurve is a many trousered thing...'

Also available on tape and CD:

'...and that's when it fell off in my hand.'

'...then he ate my boy entrancers.'

'...startled by his furry shorts!'

'Luuurve is a many trousered thing...'

Angus, thongs and full-frontal snogging

and full-

frontal snogging

You'll laugh
your knickers off!

Louise Rennison

HarperCollins *Children's Books*

This edition produced for The Book People Ltd,
Hall Wood Avenue, Haydock, St Helens, WA11 9UL

Find out more about Georgia at www.georgianicolson.com

First published in Great Britain by Piccadilly Press Ltd, 1999
Published by Scholastic Ltd, 2001
This edition published by HarperCollins *Children's Books,* 2005
HarperCollins *Children's Books* is a division of HarperCollins*Publishers* Ltd,
77-85 Fulham Palace Road, Hammersmith, London W6 8JB

The HarperCollins *Children's Books* website address is
www.harpercollinschildrensbooks.co.uk

1

ISBN 978-0-00-782485-4

Printed and bound in England by
Clays Ltd, St Ives plc

Mixed Sources
Product group from well-managed
forests and other controlled sources
www.fsc.org Cert no. SW-COC-1806
© 1996 Forest Stewardship Council

FSC is a non-profit international organisation established to promote the
responsible management of the world's forests. Products carrying the FSC
label are independently certified to assure consumers that they come
from forests that are managed to meet the social, economic and
ecological needs of present and future generations.

Find out more about HarperCollins and the environment at
www.harpercollins.co.uk/green

To Mutti and Vati and my little sister, also to Angus. His huge furry outside may have gone to cat heaven, but the scar on my ankle lingers on. Also to Brenda and Jude and the fab gang at Piccadilly. And thanks to John Nicolson.

La marche avec mystery

Sunday August 23rd
My Bedroom
Raining
10:00 a.m.

Dad had Uncle Eddie round so naturally they had to come and nose around and see what I was up to. If Uncle Eddie (who is bald as a coot – too coots, in fact) says to me one more time, "Should bald heads be buttered?" I may kill myself. He doesn't seem to realise that I no longer wear romper-suits. I feel like yelling at him. "I am fourteen years old, Uncle Eddie! I am bursting with womanhood, I wear a bra! OK, it's a bit on the loose side and does ride up round my neck if I run for the bus... but the womanly potential is there, you bald coot!"

Talking of breasts, I'm worried that I may end up like the

rest of the women in my family, with just the one bust, like a sort of shelf affair. Mum can balance things on hers when her hands are full – at parties, and so on, she can have a sandwich and drink and save a snack for later by putting it on her shelf. It's very unattractive. I would like a proper amount of breastiness but not go too far with it, like Melanie Griffiths, for instance. I got the most awful shock in the showers after hockey last term. Her bra looks like two shopping bags. I suspect she is a bit unbalanced hormonally. She certainly is when she tries to run for the ball. I thought she'd run right through the fence with the momentum of her "bosoomers" as Jas so amusingly calls them.

Still in my room
Still raining
Still Sunday
11:30 a.m.
I don't see why I can't have a lock on my bedroom door. I have no privacy: it's like *Noel's House Party* in my room. Every time I suggest anything around this place people start shaking their heads and tutting. It's like living in a house full of chickens dressed in frocks and trousers. Or a house full of

those nodding dogs, or a house full of... anyway... I can't have a lock on my door is the short and short of it.

"Why not?" I asked Mum reasonably (catching her in one of the rare minutes when she's not at Italian evening class or at another party).

"Because you might have an accident and we couldn't get in," she said.

"An accident like what?" I persisted.

"Well... you might faint," she said.

Then Dad joined in, "You might set fire to your bed and be overcome with fumes."

What is the matter with people? I know why they don't want me to have a lock on my door, it's because it would be a first sign of my path to adulthood and they can't bear the idea of that because it would mean they might have to get on with their own lives and leave me alone.

Still Sunday
11:35 a.m.

There are six things very wrong with my life:

1. I have one of those under-the-skin spots that will never come to a head but lurk in a red way for the

♥ 9

next two years.

2. It is on my nose.
3. I have a three-year-old sister who may have peed somewhere in my room.
4. In fourteen days the summer hols will be over and then it will be back to Stalag 14 and Oberführer Frau Simpson and her bunch of sadistic "teachers".
5. I am very ugly and need to go into an ugly home.
6. I went to a party dressed as a stuffed olive.

11:40 a.m.

OK, that's it. I'm turning over a new leaf. I found an article in Mum's *Cosmo* about how to be happy if you are very unhappy (which I am). The article is called "Emotional confidence". What you have to do is *Recall... Experience... and HEAL.* So you think of a painful incident and you remember all the ghastly detail of it... this is the Recall bit, then you experience the emotions and acknowledge them and then you JUST LET IT GO.

2:00 p.m.

Uncle Eddie has gone, thank the Lord. He actually asked me if I'd like to ride in the sidecar on his motorbike. Are all adults from Planet Xenon? What should I have said? "Yes, certainly, Uncle Eddie, I would like to go in your pre-war sidecar and with a bit of luck all of my friends will see me with some mad, bald bloke and that will be the end of my life. Thank you."

4:00 p.m.
Jas came round. She said it took her ages to get out of her catsuit after the fancy dress party. I wasn't very interested but I asked her why out of politeness.

She said, "Well, the boy behind the counter in the hire shop was really good-looking."

"Yes, so?"

"Well, so I lied about my size – I got a size ten catsuit instead of twelve."

She showed me the marks around her neck and waist: they are quite deep. I said, "Your head looks a bit swollen up."

"No, that's just Sunday."

I told her about the *Cosmo* article and so we spent a few hours recalling the fancy dress party (i.e. the painful incident) and experiencing the emotions in order to heal them.

I blame Jas entirely. It may have been my idea to go as a stuffed olive but she didn't stop me like a pal should do. In fact, she encouraged me. We made the stuffed olive costume out of chicken wire and green crêpe paper – that was for the "olive" bit. It had little shoulder straps to keep it up and I wore a green T-shirt and green tights underneath. It was the "stuffed" bit that Jas helped with mostly. As I recall, it was she that suggested I use Crazy Colour to dye my hair and head and face and neck red... like a sort of pimento. It was, I have to say, quite funny at the time. Well, when we were in my room. The difficulty came when I tried to get out of my room. I had to go down the stairs sideways.

When I did get to the door I had to go back and change my tights because my cat Angus had one of his "Call of the Wilds" episodes.

He really is completely bonkers. We got him when we went on holiday to Loch Lomond. On the last day I found him wandering around the garden of the guest house we were staying in. Tarry-a-Wee-While, it was called. That should give you some idea of what the holiday was like.

I should have guessed all was not entirely well in the cat department when I picked him up and he began savaging my cardigan. But he was such a lovely looking kitten, all tabby and long-haired, with huge yellow eyes. Even as a kitten he looked like a small dog. I begged and pleaded to take him home.

"He'll die here, he has no mummy or daddy," I said plaintively.

My dad said, "He's probably eaten them." Honestly, he can be callous. I worked on Mum and in the end I brought him home. The Scottish landlady did say she thought he was probably mixed breed, half domestic tabby and half Scottish wildcat. I remember thinking, Oh, that will be exotic. I didn't realise that he would grow to the size of a small Labrador only mad. I used to drag him around on a lead but, as I explained to Mrs Next Door, he ate it.

Anyway, sometimes he hears the call of the Scottish highlands. So, as I was passing by as a stuffed olive he leaped out from his concealed hiding-place behind the curtains (or his lair, as I suppose he imagined it in his cat brain) and attacked my tights or "prey". I couldn't break his hold by banging his head because he was darting from side to side. In the end I managed to reach the outdoor brush by the door and beat him off with it.

Then I couldn't get in Dad's Volvo. Dad said, "Why don't you take off the olive bit and we'll stick it in the boot."

Honestly, what is the point? I said, "Dad, if you think I am sitting next to you in a green T-shirt and tights, you're mad."

He got all shirty like parents do as soon as you point out how stupid and useless they are. "Well, you'll have to walk, then... I'll drive along really slowly with Jas and you walk alongside."

I couldn't believe it. "If I have to walk, why don't Jas and I both walk there and forget about the car?"

He got that stupid, tight-lipped look that dads get when they think they are being reasonable. "Because I want to be sure of where you are going. I don't want you out wandering the streets at night."

Unbelievable! I said, "What would I be doing walking the streets at night as a stuffed olive... gatecrashing cocktail parties?"

Jas smirked but Dad got all outraged parenty. "Don't you speak to me like that, otherwise you won't go out at all."

What is the point?

When we did eventually get to the party (me walking

next to Dad's Volvo driving at five miles an hour), I had a horrible time. Everyone laughed at first but then more or less ignored me. In a mood of defiant stuffed oliveness I did have a dance by myself but things kept crashing to the floor around me. The host asked me if I would sit down. I had a go at that but it was useless. In the end I was at the gate for about an hour before Dad arrived, and I did stick the olive bit in the boot. We didn't speak on the way home.

Jas, on the other hand, had a great time. She said she was surrounded by Tarzans and Robin Hoods and James Bonds. (Boys have very vivid imaginations... not.)

I was feeling a bit moody as we did the "recall" bit. I said bitterly, "Well, I could have been surrounded by boys if I hadn't been dressed as an olive."

Jas said, "Georgia, you thought it was funny and I thought it was funny but you have to remember that boys don't think girls are for funniness."

She looked annoyingly "wise" and "mature". What the hell did she know about boys? God, she had an annoying fringe. Shut up, fringey.

I said, "Oh yeah, so that's what they want, is it? Boys? They want simpering girly-wirlys in catsuits?"

Through my bedroom window I could see next door's poodle leaping up and down at our fence, yapping. It would be trying to scare off our cat Angus... fat chance.

Jas was going on and on wisely. "Yes they do, I think they do like girls who are a bit soft and not so, well... you know."

She was zipping up her rucksack. I looked at her. "Not so what?" I asked.

She said, "I have to go, we have an early supper."

As she left my room I knew I should shut up. But you know when you should shut up because you really should just shut up... but you keep on and on anyway? Well, I had that.

"Go on... not so what?" I insisted.

She mumbled something as she went down the stairs.

I yelled at her as she went through the door, "Not so like me you mean, don't you?!!!"

11:00 p.m.
I can already feel myself getting fed up with boys and I haven't had anything to do with them yet.

Midnight

Oh God, please, please don't make me have to be a lesbian like Hairy Kate or Miss Stamp.

12:10 a.m.

What do lesbians do, anyway?

Monday August 24th

5:00 p.m.

Absolutely no phonecalls from anyone. I may as well be dead. I'm going to have an early night.

5:30 p.m.

Libby came in and squiggled into bed with me, saying, "Hahahahaha!" for so long I had to get up. She's so nice, although a bit smelly. At least she likes me and doesn't mind if I have a sense of humour.

7:00 p.m.

Ellen and Julia rang from a phonebox. They took turns to speak in French accents. We're going for a mystery walk tomorrow. Or *La Marche Avec Mystery*.

10:30 p.m.

Have put on a face mask made from egg yolk just in case we see any *les garçons gorgeous* on our walk.

Tuesday August 25th

9:00 a.m.

Woke up and thought my face was paralysed. It was quite scary – my skin was all tight and stiff and I couldn't open my eyes properly. Then I remembered the egg-yolk mask. I must have fallen asleep reading. I don't think I'll go to bed early again, it makes my eyes go all puffy. I look like there is a touch of the Oriental in my family. Sadly not the case. The nearest we have to any exotic influence is Auntie Kath, who can sing in Chinese, but only after a couple of pints of wine.

11:00 a.m.

Arranged to rendezvous with Ellen and Julia at Whiteleys so we can start our *La Marche Avec Mystery*. We agreed we would dress "sports casual" so I'm wearing ski trousers, ankle boots and a black top with a roll neck, with a PVC jacket. I'm going for the young Brigitte Bardot look which is a shame as, a) I am nothing like her and b) I haven't got blonde hair, which is, as we all know, her trademark. I would have blonde hair if I was allowed but it honestly is like *Playschool* at my house. My dad has got the mentality of a Teletubby only not so developed. I said to Mum, "I'm going to dye my hair blonde, what product would you recommend?" She pretended not to hear me and went on dressing Libby. But Dad went ballistic.

"You're fourteen years old, you've only had that hair for fourteen years and you want to change it already! How bored are you going to be with it by the time you are thirty? What colour will you be up to by then?"

Honestly, he makes little real sense these days. I said to Mum, "Oh, I thought I could hear a voice squeaking and making peculiar noises, but I was mistaken. TTFN."

As I ran for the door I heard him shouting, "I suppose you think being sarcastic and applying eyeliner in a straight line will get you some O-levels!!!"

O-levels, I ask you. He's a living reminder of the Stone Age.

Noon
La Marche Avec Mystery. We walked up and down the High

Street, only speaking French. I asked passers-by for directions, "*Où est la gare, s'il vous plaît?*" and "*Au secours, j'oublie ma tête, aidez-moi, s'il vous plaît.*"

Then... this really dishy bloke came along... Julia and Ellen wouldn't go up to him but I did. I don't know why, but I developed a limp as well as being French. He had really nice eyes... he must have been about nineteen, anyway I hobbled up to him and said, "*Excusez-moi. Je suis Française. Je ne parle pas l'anglais. Parlez-vous Français?*"

Fortunately he looked puzzled, it was quite dreamy. I pouted my mouth a bit. Cindy Crawford said that if you put your tongue behind your back teeth when you smile, it makes your smile really sexy. Impossible to talk, of course, unless you like sounding like a loony.

Anyway, dreamboat said, "Are you lost? I don't speak French."

I looked puzzled (and pouty). "*Au secours, monsieur,*" I breathed.

He took my arm. "Look, don't be frightened, come with me."

Ellen and Jools looked amazed: he was bloody gorgeous and he was taking me somewhere. I hobbled along attractively by his side. Not for very long, though, just into a French pâtisserie where the lady behind the counter was French.

8:00 p.m.
In bed.

The French woman talked French at me for about forty years. I nodded for as long as humanly possible then just ran out of the shop and into the street. The gorgeous boy looked surprised that my limp had cured itself so quickly.

I really will have to dye my hair now if I ever want to go shopping in this town again.

Wednesday August 26th

11:00 a.m.

I have no friends. Not one single friend. No one has rung, no one has come round. Mum and Dad have gone to work, Libby is at playschool. I may as well be dead.

Perhaps I am dead. I wonder how you would know? If you died in your sleep and woke up dead, who would let you know?

It could be like in that film where you can see everyone but they can't see you because you are dead. Oh, I've really given myself the creeps now... I'm going to put on a really loud CD and dance about.

Noon

Now I am still freaked out but also tired. If I did die I wonder if anyone would really care. Who would come to my funeral? Mum and Dad, I suppose... they'd have to as it's mostly their fault that I was depressed enough to commit suicide in the first place.

Why couldn't I have a normal family like Julia and Ellen? They've got normal brothers and sisters. Their dads have got beards and sheds. My mum won't let my dad have a shed since he left his fishing maggots in there and it became bluebottle headquarters.

When the electrician came because the fridge had blown up he said to Mum, "What madman wired up this fridge? Is there someone you know who really doesn't like you?" And Dad had done the wiring. Instead of DIY he talks about feelings and stuff. Why can't he be a real dad? It's pathetic in a grown man.

I don't mean I want to be like an old-fashioned woman – you know, all lacy and the man is all tight-lipped and never says anything even if he has got a brain tumour. I want my boyfriend (provided, God willing, I am not a lesbian) to be emotional... but only about me. I want him to be like Darcy in *Pride and Prejudice* (although, having said that, I've seen him in other things like *Fever Pitch* and he's not so sexy out of frilly shirts and tights). Anyway, I'll never have a boyfriend because I am too ugly.

2:00 p.m.
Looking through the old family albums... I'm not really surprised I'm ugly, the photos of Dad as a child are terrifying. His nose is huge... it takes up half of his face. In fact, he is literally just a nose with legs and arms attached.

10:00 p.m.
Libby has woken up and insists on sleeping in my bed. It's quite nice, although she does smell a bit on the hamsterish side.

Midnight
The tunnel of love dream I've just had, where this gorgey bloke is carrying me through the warm waters of the

Caribbean, turns out to be Libby's wet pyjamas on my legs.

Change bed. Libby not a bit bothered and in fact slaps my hand and calls me "Bad boy" when I change her pyjamas.

Thursday August 27th

11:00 a.m.

I've started worrying about what to wear for first day back at school. It's only eleven days away now. I wonder how much "natural" make-up I can get away with? Concealer is OK – I wonder about mascara. Maybe I should just dye my eyelashes? I hate my eyebrows. I say eyebrows but in fact it's just the one eyebrow right along my forehead. I may have to do some radical plucking if I can find Mum's tweezers. She hides things from me now because she says that I never replace anything. I'll have to rummage around in her bedroom.

1:00 p.m.

Prepared a light lunch of sandwich spread and milky coffee. There's never anything to eat in this house. No wonder my elbows stick out so much.

2:00 P.M.

Found the tweezers eventually. Why Mum would think I wouldn't find them in Dad's tie drawer I really don't know. I did find something very strange in the tie drawer as well as the tweezers. It was a sort of apron thing in a special box. I hope against hope that my dad is not a transvestite. It would be more than flesh and blood could stand if I had to "understand" his feminine side. And me and Mum and Libby have to watch whilst he clatters around in one of Mum's nighties and fluffy mules... We'll probably have to start calling him Daphne.

God, it's painful plucking. I'll have to have a little lie down. The pain is awful, it's made my eyes water like mad.

2:30 P.M.

I can't bear this. I've only taken about five hairs out and my eyes are swollen to twice their normal size.

4:00 P.M.

Cracked it. I'll use Dad's razor.

4:05 p.m.

Sharper than I thought. It's taken off a lot of hair just on one stroke. I'll have to even up the other one.

4:16 p.m.

Bugger it. It looks all right, I think, but I look very surprised in one eye. I'll have to even up the other one now.

6:00 p.m.

Mum nearly dropped Libby when she saw me. Her exact words were, "What in the name of God have you done to yourself, you stupid girl?"

God I hate parents! Me stupid?? They're so stupid. She wishes I was still Libby's age so she could dress me in ridiculous hats with earflaps and ducks on. God, God, God!!!

7:00 p.m.

When Dad came in I could hear them talking about me.

"Mumble mumble... she looks like... mumble mumble," from Mum, then I heard Dad, "She WHAT??? Well... mumble... mumble... grumble..." Stamp, stamp, bang, bang on the door.

"Georgia, what have you done now?"

I shouted from under the blankets – he couldn't get in because I had put a chest of drawers in front of the door – "At least I'm a real woman!!!"

He said through the door, "What in the name of arse is that supposed to mean?"

Honestly, he can be so crude.

10:00 p.m.
Maybe they'll grow back overnight. How long does it take for eyebrows to grow?

Friday August 28th
11:00 a.m.
Eyebrows haven't grown back.

11:15 a.m.
Jas phoned and wanted to go shopping – there's some new make-up range that looks so natural you can't tell you have got any on.

I said, "Do they do eyebrows?"

She said, "Why? What do you mean? Do you mean false eyelashes?"

I said, "No, I mean eyebrows. You know, the hairy bits above your eyes." Honestly friends can be thick.

"Of course they don't do eyebrows. Everyone's got eyebrows, why would you need a spare pair?"

I said, "I haven't got any any more. I shaved them off by mistake."

She said, "I'm coming round now, don't do anything until I get there."

Noon

When I open the door Jas just looks at me like I'm a Klingon. "You look like a Klingon," she says. She really is a dim friend. It's more like having a dog than a friend, actually.

6:00 p.m.

Jas has gone. Her idea of help was to draw some eyebrows on with eyeliner pencil.

Obviously I have to stay in now for ever.

7:00 p.m.

Dad is annoying me so much. He just comes to the door, looks in and laughs, and then he goes away... for a bit. He brought Uncle Eddie upstairs for a look. What am I? A daughter or a fairground attraction? Uncle Eddie said, "Never mind, if they don't grow back you and I can go into showbiz. We can do a double act doing impressions of billiard balls." Oh how I laughed. Not.

8:00 p.m.
The only nice person is Libby. She was stroking where my eyebrows used to be and then she went off and brought me a lump of cheese. Great. I have become ratwoman.

I wonder who our form teacher will be?

Pray God it's not Hawkeye Heaton. I don't want her to be constantly reminded of the unfortunate locust incident. Who would have thought a few locusts could eat so much in so little time? When I let them out into the biology lab for a bit of a fly round I wouldn't have expected them to eat the curtains.

Strikes me that Hawkeye has very little sense of humour. She is also about a hundred and a Miss – which speaks volumes in my book. Mind you, as ratwoman I'll probably end up as a teacher of biology in some poxy girls' school. Like her. Having cats and warm milk. Wearing huge knickers. Listening to the radio. Being interested in things.

I may as well kill myself. I would if I could be bothered but I'm too depressed.

Saturday August 29th
10:00 a.m.
M and D went out to town to buy stuff. Mum said did I want her to buy some school shoes for me? I glanced meaningfully at her shoes. It's sad that someone of her mature years tries to keep up with us young ones. You'd think she'd be ashamed to be mutton dressed as lamb, but no. I could see her knickers when she sat down the other day (and I wasn't the only one).

11:00 a.m.
Phone rang. Ellen and Julia and Jas are coming round after they've been to town. Apparently Jas has seen someone in a shop that she really likes. I suppose this is what life will be like for me – never having a boyfriend, always just living through others.

Noon
I was glancing through *Just 17* and it listed kissing

techniques. What I don't understand is how do you know when to do it, and how do you know which side to go to? You don't want to be bobbing around like pigeons for hours but I couldn't tell much from the photos. I wish I had never read it, it has made me more nervous and confused than I was before. Still, why should I care? I am going to be staying in for the rest of my life. Unless some gorgeous boy loses his way and wanders into my street and then finds his way up the stairs into my bedroom with a blindfold on I am stuck between these four walls for ever.

12:15 p.m.
Perhaps as I can't go out I can use my time wisely. I may tidy my room and put all my dresses in one part of my wardrobe, and so on.

12:17 p.m.
I hate housework.

12:18 p.m.
If I marry or, as is more likely, become a high-flying executive lesbian, I am never going to do housework. I will

have to have an assistant. I have no talent for tidying. Mum thinks that I deliberately ignore the obvious things but the truth is I can't tell the difference between tidy and not tidy. When Mum says, "Will you just tidy up the kitchen?" I look around and I think, Well, there's a few pans on the side, and so on, but I think it looks OK. And then the row begins.

2:00 p.m.
Putting the coffee on for the girls. It's instant but if you mix the coffee with sugar in the cup for ages it goes into a sort of paste, then you add water and it's like espresso. It makes your arms ache like billy-o, though.

7:00 p.m.
Brilliant afternoon! We tried all different make-ups. I've been Sellotaping my fringe to make it longer and straighter and to cover up the space where my eyebrows were. Jas said, "It makes you look like you've escaped from the funny lads' home." Ellen says if I emphasise my mouth and eyes then attention will be drawn away from my nose. So it's heavy lippy for me from now on.

We were all lolling about on my bed, listening to the Top

Forty and Jas told us about the gorgeous boy in the shop. She knows he is called Tom because someone called him Tom in the shop he works in. Supersleuth! We all pledged that we would wait until I can go out again and then we will go and look at him.

Talk then turned to kissing. Ellen said, "I went to a Christmas party at my cousin's last year and this boy from Liverpool was there. I think he was a sailor. Anyway, he was nineteen or something, and he brought some mistletoe over and he kissed me."

We were full-on, attention-wise. I said, "What was it like?"

Ellen said, "A bit on the wet side, like a sort of warm jelly feeling."

Jas said, "Did he have his lips closed or open?"

Ellen thought. "A bit open."

I asked, "Did his tongue pop out?"

Ellen said, "No, just his lips."

I wanted to know what she did with her tongue.

"Well, I just left it where it normally is."

I persisted, "What about your teeth?"

Ellen was a bit exasperated. "Oh, yeah, I took those out."

I looked a bit hurt. You know, like, I was only asking...

She said, "I can't really remember. It was a bit tickly and it didn't last long, but I liked it, I think. He was quite nice but he had a girlfriend and I suppose he thought I was just a little thirteen-year-old who hadn't been around much."

I said, "He was right."

10:00 p.m.

My sister Libby kisses me on the mouth quite a lot, but I don't think sisters count. Unless I am a lesbian, in which case it's all good practice probably.

11:00 p.m.

Through my curtains I can see a big yellow moon. I'm thinking of all the people in the world who will be looking at that same moon.

I wonder how many of them haven't got any eyebrows?

Sunday August 30th

11:00 a.m.

Thank God they're all actually going out. At last. What is all this happy family nonsense? All this "we should do things as a family"?

As I pointed out to Dad, "We are four people who, through great misfortune, happen to be stuck in the same house. Why make it worse by hanging around in garden centres or going for a walk together?"

Anyway, ratwoman does not go out. She just hangs around in her bedroom for the next forty years to avoid being laughed at by strangers.

I will never ever have a boyfriend. It's not fair, there are some really stupid people and they get boyfriends. Zoe Ball gets really nice boyfriends and she has got sticky-out ears.

1:00 p.m.
I still haven't tackled Dad about his apron.

1:15 p.m.
God I'm bored. I can see Mr and Mrs Next Door in their greenhouse. What do people do in them? If I end up with someone like Mr Next Door I will definitely kill myself. He has the largest bottom I have ever seen. It amazes me he can get in the greenhouse. One day his bottom will be so large

35

he will have to live in the greenhouse and have bits of chop passed to him, and so on. *O quel dommage! Sacré bleu!! Le gros monsieur dans la maison de glass!!!*

1:20 p.m.
I may start a neighbourhood newspaper.

1:22 p.m.
Oh dear. I have just seen Angus hunkering down in the long grass. He's stalking their poodle. I'll have to intervene to avert a massacre. Oh, it's OK, Mrs Next Door has thrown a brick at him.

11:00 p.m.
What a long, boring day. I hate Sundays, they are deliberately invented by people who have no life and no friends. On the plus side, I've got six o'clock shadow on the eyebrow front.

Operation Sausage

Tuesday September 1st
10:00 a.m.

Six days to school and counting. I wish my mum could be emancipated, a feminist, a working mother etc. And manage to do my ironing.

I thought I'd wear my pencil line skirt the first day back, with hold-up stockings and my ankle boots. I'm still not really resolved in the make-up department because if I do run into Hawkeye she'll make me take it off if she spots it. Then I'll get that shiny red face look which is so popular with PE teachers. On the other hand, I cannot possibly risk walking to school without make-up on. No matter how much I stick to sidestreets, sooner or later I will be bound to bump into the Foxwood lads. The biggest worry of all is the bloody beret. I must consult with the gang to see what our plan is.

5:00 p.m..

We're having an emergency Beret and Other Forms of Torture meeting tomorrow, at my place again. I have got eyebrows now but still look a bit on the startled earwig side.

7:00 p.m.

After tea, when Dad was doing the washing-up, I said casually, "Why don't you wear your special apron, Dad?"

He went ballistic and said I shouldn't be prying through his drawers. I said, "I think I've got a right to know if my dad is a transvestite."

Mum laughed, which made him even madder. "You encourage her, Connie. You show no respect, so how can she?"

Mum said, "Calm down, Bob, of course I respect you, it's just that it is quite funny to think of you as a transvestite." Then she started laughing again. Dad went off to the pub, thank goodness.

Mum said, "It's his Masonic apron. You know, that huddly duddly, pulling up one sock, I'll scratch your back if you scratch mine sort of thing."

I smiled and nodded but I haven't the remotest idea what she is talking about.

11:30 p.m.
Why couldn't I be adopted? I wonder if it's too late. Am I too old to ring Esther Rantzen's helpline? I might get Esther. Good grief.

Wednesday September 2nd
Five days to purgatory
10:00 a.m.
Oh. No, it's here already. As a special "treat" my cousin James is coming to stay with us overnight.

I mean, I used to like him and we were quite close as kids and everything, but he's so goofy now. His voice is all peculiar and he's got a funny smell. Not hamsterish like Libby but sort of doggy-cheesy. I don't think all boys smell like that, perhaps it's because he's my cousin.

2:00 p.m.
James is actually not such bad fun; he seems much younger than me and still wants to do mad dancing to old records

like we used to. We worked out some dance routines to old soul records of Mum's. "Reach out I'll be There" by the Four Tops was quite dramatic. It was two pointy points, one hand on heart, one hand on head, a shimmy and a full turn around. Sadly there's not much room in my bedroom and James trod on Angus who, as usual, went berserk.

Actually, it would be more unusual to say "Angus went calm". Anyway, he ran up the curtains and finally got on top of the door and crouched there, hissing (Angus, that is, not James). We tried to get him down and also we tried to get to the bathroom but he wouldn't let us. If we tried to get through the door he'd strike out with his huge paw. I think he is part cat, part cobra. In the end Mum got him down with some sardines.

7:00 p.m.
After "tea" James and I were listening to records and talking about what we were going to do after we ditch The Olds (as we call our parents). I'm going to be a comedy actress or someone like those "it" girls who don't actually do anything except be "it". The newspapers follow them all day and the headlines say, *Oh, look, there is Tara Pompeii Too-Booby going out to buy some biscuits!! Or Tamsin Snaggle-Tooth Polyplops*

goes skiing in fur bikini. And they just make money from that. That is me, that is.

James wants to do something electronic (whatever that means; I didn't encourage him to explain because I felt a coma coming on). He wants to travel first, though. I said, "Oh, do you, where?" Thinking... Himalayas, yak butter, opium dens, and he said, "Well, the Scilly Isles in particular."

11:00 p.m.
Something a bit weird happened. We went to bed – James slept in a sleeping bag on some cushions on the floor, and we were chatting about Pulp, and so on, and then I felt this pressure on my leg. He had reached out and held my leg. I didn't know what to do so I kept really still, so that he might think he'd just got hold of a piece of the bed or something. I stayed still for ages but then I think I must have dropped off.

Thursday September 3rd
9:00 a.m.
At last the eyebrows are starting to look normal.

♡ 41

2:00 p.m.

James went home. The "leg" incident was not mentioned. Boys are truly weird.

5:00 p.m.

Libby has the flu. She was all pale and miserable. I let her sleep in my bed and she was snuffling, poor thing. Poor little thing, I really love my little sister.

8:30 p.m.

Took Libbs some hot milk and thought she might like me to read *The Magic Faraway Tree*. She said, "Yes, now, more please," and sat herself up in my bed. Then, as I opened the book, she took my duvet cover and blew her nose on it. It's absolutely covered in green snot. Who would have thought such a tiny girl could produce a bucket of snot?

10:00 p.m.

I had to sleep in the sleeping bag. What a life.

Friday September 4th
11:00 a.m.

Emergency Beret and Other Forms of Torture meeting to be held this afternoon. I've decided that my eyebrows have recovered enough to venture out (obviously not on their own). I feel like one of those blokes who have been held in solitary in a cellar and come out into the daylight blinking.

We go to Costa Ricos for cappuccino. I hate cappuccino but everyone drinks it so you can't say no. I haven't been out for weeks – well, five days. Town looks great. Like New York... but without the skyscrapers and Americans. We decide we'll have the meeting and then go and sneak a look at the boy that Jas likes, Tom. He works in Jennings. I said, "What, the grocer's?"

Jas said, "It's a greengrocer-cum-delicatessen," and I said, "Yes, well it sells houmus." And she said, "And yoghurt," and I said, "*Quel dommage.* I forgot the yoghurt. Yes, it's like going to Paris going into that shop, apart from the turnips."

Jas sort of went red, so I thought I would shut up. Jas doesn't get angry very often but she has a hefty kick.

Jools said, "Shall we talk beret plan?" At our stupid school you have to wear a beret with your outdoor uniform.

♥ 43

It's a real pain because, as we know, everyone – and especially the French who invented it – looks like a stupid prat in a beret. And they flatten your hair. Last term we perfected a way of wearing it like a pancake. You flatten it out and then pin it with hair grips right at the back of your head. Still a pain, but you can't see it from the front. Ellen said she had made up a different method, called "the sausage". She showed us how to do it. She rolled her beret up really tight like a little sausage and then pinned it with hair grips right at the back in the centre of her head. You could hardly see it at all. It was brilliant. We decided to instigate Operation Sausage at the beginning of the term.

It has been a constant battle about these berets. The so-called grown-ups will not negotiate with us. We sent a deputation to the headmistress Slim (so-called because she weighs twenty-five stone... at least. Her feet cascade out of her shoes). At the deputation we asked why we had to wear berets. She said it was to keep standards up, and to enhance the image of the school in the community. I said, "But the boys from Foxwood call out, 'Have you got any onions?' I don't think they do respect us, I think they make a mock and a sham of us."

Slim shook herself. It was a sort of habit that she had when she was irritated with us (i.e. all the time). It made her look like a jelly with shoes on.

"Georgia, you have had my last word on this, berets are to be worn to and from school. Why not think about something a bit more important, like perhaps getting less than twenty-one poor conduct marks next term?"

Oh, go on, play the old record again. Just because I am lively.

We did have another campaign last year, which was If You Want Us to Wear Our Berets, let's Really Wear Our Berets.

This involved the whole of our year pulling their berets right down over their heads with just their ears showing. It was very stunning, seeing one hundred girls at the bus stop with just their ears showing. We stopped eventually (even though it really infuriated Slim and Hawkeye) because it was terribly hot and you couldn't see where you were going and it played havoc with your hair.

Meeting over and time for boy-stalking. Jas was a bit nervous about us all going into the shop. She's not actually spoken to Tom – well, apart from saying "Two pounds of greens".

We decided that we'd lurk casually outside and then, when she went in to be served, we'd sort of accidentally spot her and pop into the shop and say "Hi". This would be casual and give us the chance to give him the once-over and also give the (wrong) impression that Jas is a very popular person.

Jas popped to the loos to make herself look natural with panstick etc. Then she went into Jennings. I gave it five minutes and then I was the first one to walk by the shop doorway. Jas was talking to a tall, dark-haired boy in black jeans. He was smiling as he handed over some onions. Jas was a bit flushed and was twiddling with her fringe. It was a very irritating habit she had. Anyway, I stopped in my tracks and said in a tone of delight and surprise (which convinced even me), "Jas... hi! What are you doing here?" And I gave her a really warm hug (managing to say in her ear, "Leave your bloody fringe alone!").

When I stopped hugging her she said, "Hi, Georgie, I was just buying some onions," and I laughed and said, "Well, you know your onions, don't you, Jas?"

Then Ellen and Jools came in with arms outstretched and shrieking with excitement, "Jas! Jas! How lovely! Gosh, we haven't seen you for ages. How are you?"

Meanwhile, the boy Tom stood there. Jas said to him, "Oh. I'm really sorry to keep you waiting," and he just went, "It's cool," and Jas asked him how much she owed him and then she said, "Bye then, thanks," and he said, "See you later." And we were outside. When we got a few metres away we didn't say anything but sort of spontaneously all started running as fast as we could and laughing.

7:00 p.m.

Just spoken to Jas on the phone. She thinks Tom is even more gorgeous but she doesn't know whether he likes her, so we have to go through the whole thing.

I could hear Jas's dad in the background, saying, "If you are seeing each other tomorrow can't you wait and not add to my phone bill?"

Parents are all the same – all skinflints. Anyway, Jas said, "He said, 'See you later.'"

I agreed but added thoughtfully, "But he might say that to everyone, like a sort of 'See you later' sort of thing."

That upset her. "You mean you don't think he likes me?"

I said, "I didn't say that. He might never say 'See you later' unless he means, 'See you later'."

That cheered her up. "So you think he might mean 'See you later', then?"

I said, "Yes."

She was quiet for a bit; I could hear her chewing her chewing gum. Then she started again, "When is 'later', though?"

Honestly, we could be here all night. I said, "Jas, I DON'T KNOW. Why don't you decide when 'later' is?"

She stopped chewing then. "You mean I should ask him out?"

I could see my book sort of beckoning to me, saying, "Come and read me, come and read me, you know you want to." So I was firm but fair. "It's up to you, Jas, but I know what Sharon Stone would do. Goodnight."

Saturday September 5th
10:00 a.m.
Same bat time. Same bat place.

10:15 a.m.

Jas called. She wants to launch Operation Get Tom. We're going to go to Costas for more detailed planning.

10:30 a.m.

Lalalalala. Life is so fab. Lalala. I even managed to put mascara on without sticking the brush in my eye. Also I tried out my new lipliner and I think the effect definitely makes my nose look smaller. In a rare moment I shared my nose anxiety with Mum. She said, "We used to use 'shaders'. You know, light highlights and darker bits to create shadow – you could put a light line of foundation down the middle and then darker bits at the sides to sort of narrow it down." Wrong answer, Mum, the correct answer is, "You are gorgeous, Georgia, and there is nothing wrong with your nose."

I didn't say that, I didn't give her the satisfaction. Instead I said, through some toast so I could deny it if I had to, "Mum, I don't want to look like you and your friends did, I've seen the photos and no one wants to look like Abba any more."

♥ 49

11:30 a.m.

Mrs Next Door complained about Angus again. He's been frightening their poodle. She says Angus stalks it. I explained, "Well, he's a Scottish wildcat, that's what they do. They stalk their prey."

She said, "I don't really think it should be a household pet, in that case."

I said, "He's not a household pet, believe me. I have tried to train him but he ate his lead. There is only so much you can do with Angus."

Honestly, is it really my job to deal with hysterical neighbours? Why doesn't she get a bigger dog? The stupid yappy thing annoys Angus.

1:00 p.m.

I'd better be nice though, otherwise I'll be accused of being a "moody teenager" and the next thing you know it will be tap tap tap on my door and Mum saying, "Is there anything you want to talk about?" Adults are so nosy.

1:30 p.m.

Went next door and asked Mrs Fussy Knickers if she wanted

anything from the shops as I was going. She sort of hid behind the door. I must be nicer. I start out being nice and then it's like someone else takes over. Am I schizophrenic as well as a lesbian?

2:00 p.m.

Jas phones. She wants me to help her with part two of her plan to get Tom. The plan is subtle. Jas and I will pass by Jennings, and as we pass the door I will pause and then say, "Oh, Jas, I just remembered I said I'd get some apples. Hang on a minute." Then I go into the shop and buy the apples. Jas stands behind me looking attractively casual. I smile as Tom hands over the grannies (Granny Smiths) and then – and here is the masterstroke – I say, "School in two days. Back to Stalag 14. Which centre of boredom and torture do you go to?" (Meaning, which school do you go to, do you see?) Then he tells me and then we know how to accidentally bump into him.

4:00 p.m.

Well, we got to Jennings and Tom was in there – Jas went a bit swoony. He is nice-looking, I must say, with sort of crinkly hair and great shoulders. I said my "Hang on, Jas, I promised I'd get some apples," and we went in, so she could lurk attractively behind me, as planned.

When he saw her Tom looked and smiled. I asked for my grannies and he said, "Sure. Are you looking forward to going back to school?"

(Hang on a minute, those were my lines. Still, I've done drama for four years so I improvised.) I rejoined, "Does the Pope hate Catholics?"

He smiled but I didn't really mean to say anything about the Pope, it just popped out. Tom went on, "Which school do you two go to?" I was just about to tell him (even though in our plan it wasn't really his turn)... when a Sex God came out of the back room.

I swear he was so gorgeous it made you blink and open your mouth like a goldfish. He was very tall and had long, black hair and really intense, dark-blue eyes and a big mouth and was dressed all in black. (And that's all I remember, officer.) He came over to Tom and handed him a cup of tea. Tom said, "Thanks," and the Sex God spoke. "Can't let my little brother slave away, serving apples to good-looking girls without even a cup of tea." Then he

WINKED at Tom and SMILED at me, then he went out the back.

I just stood there, looking at the space where SG had been. Clutching my apples, Tom said, "That's forty pence. Did you tell me what school you both go to?"

I came out of my trance and hoped I hadn't been dribbling. "Er... I..." and I couldn't remember.

Jas looked at me as if I had gone mad and said, "Oh, it's only the one we've been at for four years, Latimer and Ridgley. Which one do you go to?"

7:00 p.m.
I am still in a state of shock. I have just met Mr Gorgeous. And he is Tom's brother. And he is gorgeous. He saw me with my mouth open. But, fortunately, not without eyebrows. Oh God! Quick, nurse, the screens!!

7:05 p.m.
I tried opening my mouth in the mirror like I imagine it looked like in the shop. It doesn't make me look very intelligent but it also doesn't make my nose look any bigger, which is a plus (of sorts).

1:00 a.m.

I wonder how old he is? I must become more mature quickly. I'll start tomorrow.

Sunday September 6th

8:00 a.m.

When I walked into the kitchen Dad dropped his cup in a hilarious (not) display of surprise that I was up so early. "What has happened, George, has your bed caught fire? Are you feverish? It's not midday yet, why are you up?"

I said, "I came down for a cup of hot water, if that's OK." (Very cleansing for the system; I must avoid a spot attack at all costs.)

Mum said, "Well, I'm off, Libby, give your big sister a kiss before we go." Libby gave me a big smacking kiss which was nice but a bit on the porridgey side. Still, I must get on.

10:00 a.m.

I have completed the *Cosmo* yoga plan for inner peace and confidence. I vow to get up an hour before school and go through the twelve positions of "Sun worship". I feel great and two or three foot taller. The Sex God will not be able to resist the new, confident, radiant, womanly me.

2:00 p.m.
Face pack done and milk bath taken. I must try and get the milk stains off the bath towel somehow, it already smells a bit sour.

Jas rang. She thinks we should track Tom tomorrow after school. Tom – what is he to me?

4:00 p.m.
Just discovered that Libby has used the last of my sanitary towels to make hammocks for her dolls.

4:30 p.m.
She has also used all of my Starkers foundation cream on her panda: its head is entirely beige now.

5:00 p.m.
I have no other foundation or money. I may have to kill her.

5:15 p.m.
No. Peace. Ohm. Inner peace.

8:00 p.m.

Aahhhh. Early to bed, early to rise.

9:30 p.m.

Woke with a start. Thought it might be time to get up.

Midnight

Should I wear my pencil skirt or not tomorrow.

Monday September 7th

8:30 a.m.

Overslept and had to race to get a lift to Jas's with my dad. No time for yoga or make-up. Oh well, I'll start tomorrow. God alone knows how the Dalai Lama copes on a daily basis. He must get up at dawn. Actually, I read somewhere that he does get up at dawn.

8:45 a.m.

Jas and I running like loonies up the hill to the school gate. I thought my head was going to explode I was so red, and also I just remembered I hadn't got my beret on. I could see Hawkeye at the school gate so no time for the sausage method. I just rammed it on my head. Bugger bugger, pant pant. As we ran up to the gate I catapulted into... the Sex God. He looked DIVINE in his uniform. He was with his mates, having a laugh and just strolling coolly along. He looked at me and said, "You're keen." I could have died.

9:00 a.m.
My only hope is that a) he didn't recognise me and b) if he did recognise me he likes the "flushed, stupid idiot" look in a girl.

9:35 a.m.
After assembly I popped into the loos and looked in the mirror. Worst fears confirmed – I am Mrs Ugly. Small, swollen eyes, hair plastered to my skull, HUGE red nose. I look like a tomato in a school uniform. Well, that is that then.

4:00 p.m.
The bell. Thank God, now I can go home and kill myself.

7:00 p.m.

In bed. Uncle Eddie says there is an unseen force at work of which we have no comprehension... Well, if there is, why is it picking on me?

Tuesday September 8th

8:00 a.m.

Still no time to do my yoga. Not that it matters any more. I did manage to do the sausage beret and the lip-gloss and the concealer. Nothing like shutting the stable door and tarting up the horse after it's bolted.

8:20 a.m.

Nice and early with Jas. This time we are both ready. We walked up the hill really chatting and laughing. Waving at friends (well actually, waving at anyone, just to give the impression that we are really popular). We walked slowly at the end bit leading up to the gate and although there was the usual crush of Foxwood boys ogling, there was no sign of Tom or SG.

9:30 a.m.

I'd forgotten how utterly crap school is. In assembly there was a bit of chatting going on before Slim took the stage, and do you know what she said? She said, "Settle, girls, settle." Like we were a bunch of pigeons or doves or something. She's already started her fascist regime by saying she has been told that some girls were not wearing their berets as they arrived at school. She would like the older girls to set an example to the younger ones, rather than the other way round. Is this what my life is now? Talking about berets? Whilst a Sex God strolls around on the planet? I felt like shouting out, in front of assembly, "Get a life, Slim!! In fact, get two... there's enough of you!!"

But Hawkeye was looking at me. I know she was thinking about the locusts. She's always watching me. She's like a stoat. I don't think I can stand much more of this and it's only nine thirty.

5:00 p.m.

What a nightmare! Jas, Ellen, Jools and I are NOT ALLOWED to sit together at the back. I CANNOT BELIEVE IT. Instead, I have been placed next to Nauseating Pamela

Green. It is more than flesh and blood can stand. Nauseating P. Green is so boring it makes you want to slit your wrists just looking at her. Plus Hawkeye is our form mistress. *Quelle horreur* and triple *merde*. And it's physics last thing Friday afternoon. What is the point?

Wednesday September 9th
8:40 a.m.
I have perfected putting a little bit of mascara on so that you can't tell I have got any on.

No sign of the lads.

1:00 p.m.
After lunch Alison Peters and Jackie Mathews came by. They were smoking and I must say they are common girls, but obviously I must not say it to them as I do not want a duffing up, or chewing gum in my tennis shoes.

Jackie said, "We're doing a new thing tomorrow, it's a sort of Aleisteir Crowley thing, so you can all come and meet us in 5C form room tomorrow after second lunch."

Cheers, thanks a lot. Good night. It is, of course, strictly forbidden to be in school after second lunch. I sense something... what is it? Oh yes, it's my first poor conduct mark coming along.

6:00 p.m.
Is my life over? Is this all there is? Downstairs my parents are laughing at something and in the other room Libby is playing with her dolls. I can hear her talking to them. It's so sad, that she is so young and she doesn't know the sadness that lies ahead. That is what is so sad. I can hear her little voice murmuring... what is she saying...?

Oh, it's "Poor Georgia, poor Georgia."

Thursday September 10th
5:00 p.m.
Boring day at school, then home to my even more boring home life. I wanted to debrief with Jas but she had to go to the dentist. Jackie and Alison's proposed Aleisteir Crowley extravaganza was put off this lunchtime, thank the Lord. The message got passed along at assembly that Jackie was off sick. She has started taking sickies very early on in term. Anyway, we are spared whatever they had in mind for a few days. I think they take drugs. Horse tranquillizers, probably.

♡ 61

Tuesday September 15th
4:30 p.m.

Absolutely no sign of SG. However, I have found out some gossip because Katie Steadman's parents know SG's parents from some naff card club the really old go to. Apparently he's called Robbie Jennings – his parents, Mr and Mrs Jennings, own the shop – the so-called greengrocer-cum-delicatessen, according to Jas. I don't normally like Katie Steadman that much. She's OK but I get the impression she thinks I am a bit on the superficial side.

She's bloody tall, I'll say that for her, and her hair is nice, but she sort of tries too hard. She puts her hand up in class, for instance. Properly, I mean. She doesn't do the putting your hand up but leaving it all floppy at the end of your arm, so it just flaps around. That is the sign of someone who is obliged to put their hand up because that is the fascist way, but isn't really putting their hand up. I have taken to putting my hand up and pointing one finger forward – you know, like at football matches when everyone points at a chubby player and chants, "Who ate all the pies?" But as usual any sign of humour is stamped down in this place. Hawkeye said, "Georgia, if you are too tired to put your hand up properly perhaps you should go to bed earlier... or perhaps a few thousand lines might strengthen your wrist?"

I may try it out on Herr Kamyer – we have him for German and physics, which is the only bright spot in this hell-hole. He has the double comedy value of being both German and the only male teacher in an all girls' school.

8:00 p.m.

Listening to classical music, I thought it might be soothing, but it's really irritating and has no proper tune.

8:05 p.m.

I love life!!! Jas has just phoned to say we've been invited to a party at Katie Steadman's and... Katie has asked Tom and Robbie. YESSSSS!!!! I must have done a good job of being nice to Katie. WHAT ON EARTH CAN I WEAR??? Emergency, emergency! It's only a couple of weeks away.

8:10 p.m.

I'd better do my yoga.

8:15 p.m.
I'd better start applying face masks now.

8:20 p.m.
I wonder if I slept with a peg on my nose, like Amy in *Little Women*, if it would make it smaller? Why couldn't Mum choose someone with a normal sized hooter to marry?

8:30 p.m.
I asked Mum why she married Dad (he was bowling with Uncle Eddie – I ask you). She thought for a bit and then she said, "He makes me laugh." He makes her laugh. He makes her laugh. Well, Bart Simpson makes me laugh, but I'm not going to marry him.

Midnight
Hahahahahahahaha.

Monday September 21st
8:00 a.m.
Eleven days to the party.

Tuesday September 22nd
9:30 a.m.
Someone farted in assembly this morning (I suspect Nauseating P. Green). Whoever it was, it was really loud and during the silence we were having to think about all the poor people. And it wasn't just a quick one, it was a knee-trembler. Jas, Ellen, Julia and me were shrieking with laughter, well everyone was. I was laughing for most of the day and now my stomach hurts.

Thursday September 24th
5:30 p.m.
In bed. I'm absolutely frozen. I may have TB. Honestly, Miss Stamp is obviously a sex pervert as well as clearly being a lesbian. Why else would anyone make girls run around in sports knickers hitting a ball with sticks? She calls it hockey – I call it the sick wanderings of a sick mind. If I miss this party because of lesbian lust Miss Stamp WILL DIE. SHE WILL DIE.

Friday September 25th
10:00 a.m.

A sighting at last!! On the way to school we saw Tom. He actually stopped to chat, he said, "Hi, having fun?"

I said, "Yes, what could be more fun than being with sadistic loonies for eight hours every day?"

He laughed and said, directly to Jas, "Are you going to Katie's party?"

Jas went all pink and white, then sort of pinky-white apart from the tip of her nose which remained red. I must remember to tell her what she looked like. She managed to reply and he said, "Well, I look forward to seeing you there."

Jas was ecstatic. "Did you hear what he said?"

"Yes."

"He said, 'Are you going to Katie's party?'"

"Yes."

"He said, 'Well, I look forward to seeing you there.'"

"Yes."

"He said, 'I look forward to seeing you there.'"

"We've been through this."

"He said, 'I look forward to seeing you there,'... to me. He said 'you' because he meant me."

"Er, Jas."

"Yes?"

"Will you shut up now?"

5:00 p.m.

She didn't though.

Herr Kamyer didn't take us for physics as he has a cold. Double damn. When am I going to have any fun? *Sacré bleu.*

Saturday September 26th

10:00 a.m.

Went for a moody autumn walk with Libby in her pushchair. She was singing, "I am the Queen, oh, I am the Queen." She wouldn't take off the fairy wings that I had made for her. It was a nightmare getting her into the pushchair. The clouds were scudding across the sky but it was quite sunny and crisp. I cheered up enough to join in the singing with Libby. We were both yelling, "I am the Queen, oh, I am the Queen!" and that's when he got out of a red mini. Robbie. The SG. He saw me and said, "Oh hello, we've met before, haven't we?"

I smiled brilliantly, trying to do it without making my

nose spread out over all my face. It's a question of relaxing the mouth, putting the tongue behind the back teeth but slightly flaring the nostrils so that they don't go wild. He looked at me a bit oddly.

"Apples," I said wittily.

"Oh yeah," he said, "the shop, you and your friend."

He smiled again. He was dreamy when he smiled. Then he bent down to Libby who, true to form, gave him one of her scary "I am a crazy child" looks. She said, "I am the queen," and he said, "Are you?" (Ooohhh, he's so lovely to children.)

Then Libby said, "Yes, I am the queen and Georgia did a big poo this morning."

I couldn't believe it. He could not believe it. Nobody could believe it. It was unbelievable, that's why. He stood up quickly and I said, "Er, well, I'd better be going."

And he said, "Yes, see you later."

And I thought, Think Sharon Stone, think Sharon Stone. So I said, "Yes, well I'll probably see you at Katie's party," and he said, "No, I'm not going, I'm doing something else that night."

7:00 p.m.

"Georgia did a big poo..."

7:05 p.m.

"No, I'm not going, I'm doing something else that night."

7:06 p.m.

Does life get any worse?

8:00 p.m.

Yes it does. Dad has just put his head round the door to say, "James is popping over tomorrow. We thought we'd all go to Stanmer Park for the day."

Sunday September 27th

10:00 p.m.

James tried to kiss me!!!

It was disgusting. He's my cousin. It's incest. I can't even think about it or I'll be sick. Erlack erlack.

10:05 p.m.

It was in my room after a *horriblement* day spent tramping

around a bloody park. How old do they think I am? They made me go on a seesaw. I, of course, snagged my new tights.

So a summary of my lovely day out is... I snagged my tights, then I was attacked by my cousin. *Perfectamondo*. In my room!!!

10:07 p.m.

When we got back James and me were listening to records and reading old joke books and suddenly he switched off the light and said, "Shall we play tickly bears?" Tickly bears!! We used to play that when we were about five. One person would be the tickly bear and they would chase the other person and tickle them and, er... that's it. I was so shocked (and also couldn't see a thing in the dark) that I just sort of went "Nnnnnnnnnn". And then he said, "Grr gotcha!" and started tickling me. It was the most embarrassing thing. But it didn't end there – a sort of wet thing touched my face near my nose. I leaped up like a salmon and stumbled for the light. James sort of stood up and then he picked up a joke book and started reading it. So I did as well. Then he got taken home by my dad. The wet

70

thing on the nose incident was never mentioned. Like the leg.

I don't think I can stand much more of this.

Monday September 28th
11:00 a.m.

At break I told Jas and Jools everything. They went, "Errgghhhlack, that's truly disgusting. Your cousin? That is sad." Jools said that she had actually seen her brother's "how's your father" quite often. She said, "it's quite nice, really, like a mouse." She lives in a world of her own (thank God). Well bless us, Tiny Tim, one and all, I say.

4:15 p.m.

On the way home. I could kill Jas. She's all excited about the party and I might as well not go now. Jackie and Alison caught up with us on the way home. Jackie had so much make-up on. And her hair was all done. As we passed the loos in the park she made us stand lookout whilst she changed out of her school uniform.

"I'm off clubbing," she said from inside the loos, mistaking me for someone who was remotely interested in what she did.

"I didn't think that clubs opened at four thirty," I said.

She called out, "Don't be dim, Ringo." (I hate her. I hate her.) "I'm off to my mate's first to get ready, put my make-up on and everything." Put her make-up on? If she put any more make-up on she'd hardly be able to hold her head up because of the weight.

She emerged in a sort of satin crop top and tight trousers: she looked about twenty-five.

"I've got a date with the DJ at Loveculture – he's so cool. I think he's about thirty but I like mature men."

After they'd gone I walked on with Jas. "Do you think that Jackie has 'done it'?" I asked her. Jas said, "Well, put it this way... is the Queen Mother really, really old?" Sometimes Jas is quite exceptionally mad. Just to prove my point she went on, "Gemma Crawford was telling me that she knows a boy who gives kissing lessons. Do you think we should go before the party?"

I just looked at her. "Jas, are you suggesting that we go to a male prostitute?"

Jas went on, "He only does kissing and you don't pay."

I just tutted.

10:00 p.m.

I lay on my arm until it went numb and then I lifted it (with the non-numb arm) on to my breasts. I wanted to see what it felt like to have a strange hand on them. It was quite nice, but what do I know? I'm too full of strange urges to think properly. Should I wear my bra to the party?

10:05 p.m.

Urgh, it's horrible when the feeling starts coming back into your arm when it's been numb.

11:07 p.m.

Kissing the back of your hand is no good because you can't tell which is which – which is lip and which is hand – so you don't get a proper sensation from either. Do boys have this trouble or do they just know how to do stuff?

11:15 p.m.

No, is the answer, if the "tickly bear" incident is anything to go by.

Tuesday September 29th

8:30 a.m.

Biology, double maths, Froggie and geoggers. *Qu-est ce que le point?*

In my room

6:00 p.m.

What a fiasco. Jackie and Alison decided that today was the day for the Aleisteir Crowley fandango in the 5C form room.

It's amazing how few people stand up to them, including the teachers.

We all trooped up to 5C after second lunch. This in itself is a fiasco – you have to lurk outside the main door until the coast is clear, then dart to the downstairs loo, check if the coast is clear, then leap up the stairs to floor one and so on, up to the fifth floor.

I was shattered by the time I got up there. There were seven of us all in peak condition – i.e. spluttering and coughing. Jackie said we were going to do a black art act of levitation, calling on the dark forces to help us. Oh goodie, we're summoning the devil. What larks.

Why, I thought, oh why am I here? Maybe if we are going

to be forced to commune with the devil I could strike some sort of bargain with him, swap my dad's soul in exchange for bigger breasts for the party on Friday.

Abby Nicols "volunteered" to be the sacrificed one and she had to lie down on a desk. Jackie went at her head and Alison at her feet and then the rest of us spread out evenly around her. Jackie said, "Please be very quiet and concentrate, we are summoning dark forces. Put one finger of each hand underneath Abby's body and then we will begin."

We all did as we were told. Then Jackie shut her eyes and started chanting in a low, husky voice, "She's looking poorly. She's looking poorly," and we all had to repeat it after her one by one round the desk. Then she said, "She's looking worse. She's looking worse. She's looking ill. She's looking ill."

Actually, she was looking a bit peaky by this time. It went on for about five minutes as Abby's condition deteriorated. Finally Jackie whispered, "She's dying. She's dying..." We all repeated it. "She's dead. She's dead." She certainly did not look at all well and she was as stiff as a board. I couldn't see her breathing.

Then Jackie said, "Help us, oh master, to send Abby

Nicols upwards." And then she said, "Lift her up," and it was really freaky-deaky because I just slightly lifted with my two fingers and she sort of rose up really easily as if she was light as a feather. She was right above our heads. It was weird.

After a couple of minutes we all simultaneously got the jitters and let her down really heavily on to the desk. This seemed to perk her up a bit, because as we ran out I heard her saying, "I think I've broken my bottom."

11:00 p.m.
I woke up with a start because I heard the bedroom door open. It just opened by itself...

Wednesday September 30th
7:30 a.m.
I can't move my head from side to side because I sat up in bed all night and I have cricked it now.

1:00 p.m.
Gemma said her friend Peter Dyer, the professional kisser, is going to be around tomorrow after school. All you have to do is go to his house and knock on the door after four thirty

and before six thirty when his parents get home. Apparently it's first come first served. Has it come to this? No it has not.

9:30 p.m.
Had to discuss again with Jas what she is going to wear on Friday. She can go in the nuddy-pants for all I care.

Tainted love

Thursday October 1st

4:30 p.m.

For some reason I found myself outside Peter Dyer's house and knocking on his door. Ellen and Jas, Jools, Patty, Sarah and Mabs were all hiding behind the hedge at the bottom of the garden. What is the matter with me? I am DESPERATE – that's what the matter is.

I didn't know whether to wear lipstick or not. I don't know what the point would be if it was just going to come off... What am I saying?

4:31 p.m.

Peter opened the door. He's about seventeen and blond, sort of sleepy-looking, not unattractive in a sort of Boyzone way. I notice he is chewing gum. I hope he takes it out, otherwise

I might choke to death. There is muffled giggling from behind the hedge. Peter hears it but doesn't seem fazed.

"Do you want to come in – er – what's your name?"

I say, "Georgia," (damn, I meant to say a false name) and we go into his house.

He has tight blue jeans on and there are those tinkly things that the Japanese have outside the doors. (Not on his jeans, obviously – on the door.) You know... wind chimes. Why do they do that? It's such an annoying noise and do you really need to know that the wind is blowing? We're doing Japan in geography and to annoy Hawkeye I have memorised the islands. Hokkaido, Honshu... er, well, I nearly have. I did it last year with Northern Ireland, and reciting the counties (you remember them by the mnemonic FAT LAD – Fermanagh, Antrim, Tyrone, Londonderry, Armagh, Down) can be very impressive to trot out when you are accused of not concentrating.

Oh-oh, we are going up the stairs to Peter's room. He hasn't said a word. His room is much tidier than mine. He has made his bed, for a start. On the walls are posters of Denise van Outen and Miss December, and so on. On my walls there's a poster of Reeves and Mortimer showing their bottoms and a group shot of the cast of *Dad's Army*. Is this the big difference between girls and boys? Is this... oh-oh, Peter is sitting on his bed.

"Do you want to sit down?" he says, patting the bed.

I think, No thanks, I would rather put my head in a bag of eels, but I say, "OK," and sit down.

He puts his arm round me. I think of putting my arm round him like a hilarious Morecambe and Wise joke but I don't because I remember the stuffed olive incident. Then, with his other hand, Peter turns my face towards his. It's a good job he didn't try that yesterday when I had rigor mortis of the head. Then he says, "Close your eyes and relax."

9:00 p.m.
Phew, I suppose I am a woman now. Libby doesn't seem to realise as she has made me wear her deely-boppers to bed. She is insisting I am a huge bee. If I say, "Look, it's your bedtime now," she just goes, "Bzzzz bzzz," and looks cross.

I have to say, "Bz bz bzzy buzz buzz," and point at her bed with my feelers before she will go.

9:20 p.m.

When I got home neither Mum nor Dad seemed to notice the change in me. Mind you, I'd have to walk in with my head under my arm before Dad would get out of his chair. He's getting very chunky. I may mention it in a caring way. Anyway, as I said, phew.

When I closed my eyes Peter said, "We're going to do an ordinary kiss first." Then he kissed me. We started off with number one kissing, which is just lips, not moving. He said I was a natural, not too "firm" or toothy, which is apparently very common.

He told me how to know which side to go to (you sort of watch where the boy is going and then you fit in). Then we did a bit of movement and he told me what to do with my hands (waist is safest).

Oh, we got through a lot in half an hour. We did a bit of tongues, which was the bit I was most scared of, but actually it wasn't too bad, a bit like a little lizard tongue darting about. Cute really, in a bizarre way. The main thing to do is to strike a happy balance between "yielding" and "giving". Peter says you can take a horse to water but you can't make it kiss properly.

At the end of the session (he had a little alarm clock) he shook my hand and saw me to the door. I passed Mabs on the way out – it was her turn. I was glad that I had gone first. Jools and Ellen and Jas tried to pump me on the way home but I said, in a dignified sort of way, "I think I'd just like to think about this for a while, if you don't mind. *Bon soir.*"

10:45 p.m.
Hahahahahahahaha. I'm a natural.

Friday October 2nd
4:00 p.m.
Party time!!! I don't know why I'm so excited as SG is not even going to be there. But maybe I'll be able to try out my new snogging skills.

Jackie Mathews has got a huge lovebite on her neck. She's put about six centimetres of concealer on it and is wearing a scarf... how inconspicuoso!! It's HUGE! What has she been snogging with – a calf? I think it is so common. Why would you let someone bite you?

The day dragged by. I really am going to complain about

Miss Stamp – she should be working in a prison. I'm sure she has done before. Even though it was icy outside she insisted that in our games period we ran round the hockey pitch. You could see your breath. She found Jackie and Alison hiding in the showers having a fag and made them change into their sports knickers and do the circuit twice. Which is almost a reason to have her as a teacher. It was hilarious! Jackie might look OK when she's all dolled up in some dark nightclub, but you should see her from behind in big navy knickers!!

4:15 p.m.
Only three hours to get ready and made up before I meet Jas, Jools and Ellen and the gang at the clock tower. We're going to arrive together. Dad is insisting on picking me up at midnight. It's useless arguing with him, he'll only say, "You're lucky, in my day... blah blah blah," and then we'll be back in the Middle Ages or the seventies as he calls it.

7:30 p.m.
Meet the gang. We look like a group of funeral directors going out for a drink. Black is our new black. Katie

Steadman's house is quite posh – she has her own room as well as a bedroom. Shagpile carpets all rolled up round the walls, for dancing.

When we arrived there were about thirty people there already, including Tom. Cue Jas going all dithery and daft. He was in a group but he came over to talk to us straight away. I left Jas to it and circulated. It was good fun. I had a mad dancing phase for about an hour. I suppose I was vaguely looking for substitute snoggers for SG, but all the boys seemed a bit on the nice but goofy side. There were one or two most unfortunate skin complaints. I feel lucky just getting the odd lurker – some people looked like they had mountain ranges of spots on their faces... and some down their backs too... *Au secours!!!!*

Then I saw Peter Dyer. I waved at him and he came over. He had been talking to Katie Steadman and she seemed a bit miffed when he came over to me. Peter said, "Hi!" and I said, "Hi... er... thanks for the other day. It was really... er... great. I learned a lot. Thanks."

He looked at me sideways and stood quite close. "There was something I didn't have time to show you, come with me." And he took hold of my hand and led me out of the room. We hadn't done hand-holding but I improvised... not too floppy but not too gripping. I don't think anyone besides Katie saw us go, they were too busy dancing stupidly to a Slade record.

We went outside into the garden and went behind a big tree just by the path. Peter started kissing me (he didn't seem to be a big talker).

There was a lot more tongue business. It was all right but it was making my jaw ache a bit. Peter seemed to like it quite a lot more than I did because he sort of moaned and pushed me against the tree. Then Peter started nuzzling my neck and I thought, Oh, we haven't done necks before, he's branching out a bit, and then I nearly choked to death trying not to laugh (up against a tree... branching out, do you get it?)... but I stopped myself. You have to keep reminding yourself about boys not liking a laugh. Then I heard a car door slam and people crunching up the drive towards us.

I stepped backwards but Peter was still attached to my neck. I tripped over a root and fell on to my bottom. Peter lost his balance and fell over on top of me and made us both go "Ooofff!". From upside down I found myself looking up at a tall blonde girl I recognised from the sixth form and, next to her... SG. He was all in black and looked really annoyed.

He said all tight-lipped, "Don't you think it's about time you two went inside to the party?" I remembered the blonde's name, it was Lindsay, a notorious wet. She was looking at my legs. Probably envying them. I looked down, and noticed that my skirt had all ridden up and you could see my knickers. I wriggled it down in a "dignity at all times" sort of way, but she still smirked.

Peter said quite calmly, "Hi, Robbie, I thought you had a gig tonight."

Robbie said, "I have, but Tom forgot his key so I'm just dropping it off for him."

He didn't even glance at me or say goodbye or anything.

Midnight

I bloody hate him, big, full-of-himself type thing. Bugger bugger, double *ordure* and *merde*. What business is it of his what I do behind trees?

Tuesday October 6th

3:00 p.m.

Peter phoned me over the weekend. I don't know how he got the number because I just left in a hurry from the party. Gemma must have given it to him. Dad answered the phone, which is the end of life as we know it because HE WILL NOT LET IT LIE. He thinks it is funny and calls Peter "Your fancy man."

Peter wanted to know if I would go to the pictures next week. I said that would be great. So it looks like I have sort of got a boyfriend. Why do I feel so depressed then?

Jas is unbearable since the party. She sent me notes all through Maths.

Dear Gee-gee,

Tom is sooooo cool. He walked me home and then, when we got to the door, he gave me a really nice kiss on the cheek. His lips are really soft and he smells nice, not like my brother. He asked for my phone number – do you think he will call? What day do you think he will call?

It's Monday today and I saw him on Friday so

that is three days already. I'd call tonight if I was him, wouldn't you? Should I say yes to any day he says for a date? Or if he says Friday should I say, "Oh, sorry, I'm busy that night, and then when he says "What about Saturday?" I can say "Oh, yeah, Saturday would be cool." What do you think? Or do you think he might think I'm putting him off if I say I'm busy on Friday, so I should say yes to any day he says? Please reply quickly.
TTFN.

I've given her my worst look but she keeps sending things. I am not interested in any of the prat family Jennings.

4:00 p.m.
Sadly it makes no difference to Jas whether I am interested or not. All the way home she was telling me what Tom said or did. The more I hear about him the less I think Jas should have to do with him. All right, maybe I am being unfair and bitter, but she is my best friend and should do everything I say...

Tom wants to go into the fruit and veg business. Oh, how fascinating... Jas thinks it is.

"I think it's great that he's young but he knows where he is going."

I said brightly, "Yes, you'd never be short of potatoes."

Eventually even Jas noticed that I wasn't so keen. She looked a bit confused and said, "I thought you liked him."

I didn't say anything. All I could think of was his brother looking down at me and sort of sneering. Jas went on, "Don't you think I should go out with him?"

I still didn't say anything.

She said it again. "So you don't think I should go out with him?"

I was all enigmatic, which is not easy in a beret.

11:30 p.m.

I am a facsimile of a sham of a fax of a person. And I have a date with a professional snogger.

Midnight

Angus has eaten some of Mum's knickers. She says he'll have to go. Why can't she go, and Dad go? Or am I being unreasonable?

Thursday October 15th

Noon

Slim has put a ban on levitation. She made an announcement in assembly this morning. She was all shaky and jelly-like, her jowls were bouncing around like anything. Anyway, she said, "This school is like the back streets of Haiti. It must stop forthwith. Any girl found practising levitation will face the gravest consequences. I, for one, would not like to be in that girl's shoes."

I whispered to Ellen, "She wouldn't get in any girl's shoes. How much do you think each leg weighs? Imagine the size of her knickers... you could probably get two duvets out of them."

Then we got the eagle eye from Hawkeye for giggling.

2:00 p.m.

I feel like killing something. If I was that sort of person I'd scare a first former, as it is I will have to content myself with hiding Nauseating P. Green's pencil case.

3:00 p.m.

On my way to the science block I saw Lindsay. How wet can you be? She really is Mrs Wet. She has the wettest haircut known to humanity – all curled under at the bottom. I saw her legs in hockey and they are really spindly. Little spindly legs like she has been in a wheelchair and not been walking for years, and also when she is concentrating she wears big goggly glasses like Deirdre Barlow. I bet she keeps those well hidden when she goes out with Pratboy. Oh, hell's teeth, it's my "date" in four hours. The horrible thing is that I don't want to go. I just don't. There's nothing wrong with him or anything. I just can't be bothered somehow.

My bedroom
Midnight
I wish I'd never started this snogging business. I feel like I've been attacked by whelks. I can't see Peter any more. Why is he so keen on me, anyway? I haven't had a chance to say more than, "Er, what are you doing at GCSE...?" before I'm attacked by the whelks again. I can't go out with him any more. How can I tell him, though?

1:00 a.m.
I'll make Jas do it.

Friday October 16th
9:00 p.m.

What a week!

I got Jas to dump Peter for me. I said for her to let him down gently, so she told him that I had a personal problem. He asked what, and she said that I thought I was a lesbian. Cheers, Jas.

Monday October 19th
4:00 p.m.

It's all round school that I'm a lesbian. In games we were in the changing room and Miss Stamp came in to change out of her gear. Suddenly everyone had disappeared, leaving me on my own with her. She really has got a moustache. Does she not notice?

Friday October 23rd
8:00 p.m.

Tom phoned Jas and they're going on a "date" to watch Robbie's band. The band is called The Stiff Dylans. I bet it's crap. I bet it's *merde*. I bet it's double *merde*.

Mum and Dad were talking in the kitchen and when I

came in they stopped and looked all shifty. Don't get me wrong, I like it when they shut up when I come in, well I would like it if it had ever happened before. Mum said, "Have you ever thought you'd like to see a bit more of the world, Gee?" and I said, "If you're thinking of trying to persuade me to visit Auntie Kath in Blackpool for Christmas, you can forget it."

I can be hilariously cutting when I try.

10:00 p.m.
No matter from what angle you look at it, I do have a huge, squishy nose.

I wonder if Mum would pay for me to have plastic surgery...? If I went to the doctor and said it was psychologically damaging, to the extent that I couldn't go out or do my homework, I wonder if I could have it done on the NHS?

Then I remember to have a reality check... I don't have the George Clooney-type doctor from *ER* – the caring, incredibly good-looking face of medicine. I've got Dr Wallace, the incredibly fat, red, uncaring face of medicine. It's hard enough getting an aspirin out of him when you've got flu.

11:00 p.m.

Jas rang. She had a great time with Tom.

"Did he bring you a present, a bunch of leeks or something?" I asked meanly but Jas refused to come down from cloud nine.

She said, "No, but he's a brilliant dancer. The Stiff Dylans were ace. Robbie is a cool singer."

I had to ask in a masochistic way. "Was Lindsay there?"

Jas said, "Yes, she was, she's quite nice really, she had her hair up."

I was furious with Jas for being so disloyal and said, "Oh, it's nice that you've made new friends. I can't help thinking though, that as Lindsay's BEST friend you could advise her that people with massive ears should not wear their hair up."

I put the phone down on her.

Midnight

Qu-est ce que le point?

Monday October 26th

7:00 p.m.

I've been ignoring Jas. It's tiring, but someone has to do it.

Thursday October 29th
5:00 p.m.

In Slim's office today for a bit of a talking-to. Honestly, she has no sense of humour whatsoever.

The main difficulty is that she imagines we are at school to learn stuff and we know we are at school to fill in the idle hours before we go home and hang around with our mates doing important things. Life skills, like make-up and playing records and trapping boys.

Anyway, it was just one more little, trivial thing.

We had to have our school photo taken, all of the fourth form and the teachers together. Even including Herr Kamyer, the rogue male. Ellen and Jas, Jools and Rosie Mees and me were all in the back row because we are the tallest. Well, we've started this new craze which is based around those old TV puppet shows *Stingray* and *Supercar*. Rosie has all the old videos which we watch. We know all the key phrases like "Fire retro rockets" and "Calling International Rescue". And we walk around all stiffly like we are being worked (badly) by puppeteers. At the moment we are concentrating on Marina Aquamarina. She was part of an underwater kingdom, well her dad was the king of it, but they were being threatened by these horrible fish people (no they didn't wear codpieces but it would have been excellent if they did).

Anyway, Marina Aquamarina floated around underwater with her blonde hair trailing behind her and her arms all flopping by her side. All the boys really liked her, especially because she was dumb – when anyone spoke to her she just blinked in an appealingly dumb way. So anyway, when we are being Marina Aquamarina, as well as floating around with our arms by our sides we are not allowed to speak, just shake our heads and blink. So, for instance, if a prefect said, "Where is your beret?" you could only blink and stare and then float off quickly.

But then there is phase two, which is pretending to be a little boy in *Supercar* called Jimmy. Jimmy has a very upturned nose with freckles on it. Obviously you could just put your finger on your nose and force the tip back to get the snub nose effect but a more sophisticated method is to use egg boxes. You take one of the bits that the egg fits in and paint some nostrils on it, and some freckles, and Bob's your uncle. Pop it on some elastic and put it over your own nose. *Voilà l'enfant Jimmy!!*

So when we had the school photo done, Rosie, Ellen, Julia, Jas and me all had our Jimmynoses on. When you see the photo you don't actually notice at first, but then, when you look closely, you can see that five girls at the back all have snub noses with freckles. Bloody funny in anyone's language. Not Slim's, though. She was all of a quiver.

"Do you know how costly it is to have these photographs done? No you do not, you silly girls. Do you know how ridiculous you make yourselves and the school seem? No, you seem not to know these obvious things."

Forty years later we got let out. Our punishment is that we have to pick up all the litter in the school grounds. That should please Mr Attwood, the school caretaker. Revenge on us because we call him Elvis. He's only about one hundred and nine and the most boring, bad-tempered man in the universe, apart from my dad. I really don't know what is the matter with him lately (my dad), he's always hanging around, looking at me. Oh well, incest seems to run in my family. (That's quite a good joke, actually.)

A bit of rough

Thursday November 5th
7:00 p.m.

I hate November the fifth. On the way to school it was a nightmare of jumping-jacks and bangers. Boys are obsessed with loud noises and frightening people. I saw Peter Dyer (whelk boy) but he ignored me and also said something to his mate. He's going out with Katie Steadman now – she's welcome. I wonder if he will be my first and last boyfriend? Jas and I are talking again, which is a shame because all she wants to do is talk about Tom. She's miffed because he has to work in the shop all weekend. I said, "Well, that's what happens in the fruit and veg trade, Jas, you will always be second fiddle to his *légumes*." For once, she didn't argue back.

7:30 p.m.

Angus loves Bonfire Night. The dog next door has to be locked in a padded cell it's so frightened, but Angus loves it. He chases the rockets – he probably thinks they are grouse on fire. There's a big bonfire out on the backfields, all the street is going. I'm not, though, because I know that firelight emphasises my nose. I could wear a hat, I suppose. Is that my life, then, going around wearing a hat? No, I'll just stay in my bedroom and watch other people having fun through the window.

10:00 p.m.

Brilliant bonfire!!! I love Bonfire Night. I had baked potatoes and got chatted up by a boy from up the street. He looks a bit like Mick Jagger (although not, of course, eighty). He said, "See you around," when I left to come home. I think he might go to the thick boys' school but, hey ho, he can be my bit of rough. Snigger snigger.

Angus is curled up on my bed, which means I can't straighten my legs, but I daren't move him. He's got a singed ear and his whiskers are burnt off but he's purring.

Wednesday November 11th
4:20 p.m.

Jas comes round for a bit of a "talk" after school. I make her my special milky coffee drink. She starts to moan on. "Tom is going to be working again this weekend."

I said, "Well, I told you, it's a family business." I felt like a very wise person and also I seemed to have turned into a Jewess. I've never said "family business" in my life. *Ay vay*.

Jas didn't seem to notice my sudden Jewishness, she just raved on, "I don't know, I mean, I really, really like him but I want to have fun... I don't want to have to be all serious and think about the future and never go out."

I'd really got into the swing of my new role now. "Look, Jas, you're intelligent (see what I mean? I could say these things without any hint of sarcasm), you're a good-looking young girl, the world is at your feet. Do you want to end up with a fruit and veg man? Stay with him and the next thing you know you'll have five children and be up at dawn arguing about cabbages. Look what happened to my mum," I said meaningfully.

Jas had been following me up until that point but then

she said, "What did happen to your mum?" and I said, "She got Dad."

Jas said, "I see what you mean."

Monday November 16th
4:10 p.m.

Jas has finished with Tom. She came in all ashen-faced and swollen-eyed this morning. I had to wait until break to talk to her.

We went to the tennis courts even though it was bloody freezing. I refuse to wear a vest, though. I'm going to persevere with my bra, even if it does bunch up. I think my breasts are definitely growing. Fondling is supposed to make them bigger. Melanie Griffiths must do nothing but fondle hers, they're gigantic. Anyway, Jas told me the whole thing about Tom and how she has now become a dumper.

(Verb to dump: I dump, you dump, he/she/it dumps etc.)

Jas said, "He was upset and angry at the same time. He said he thought we were good together."

Jas looked as if she was about to cry again so I put my arm round her. Then I took it away quickly – I don't want to start the lesbian rumour again. I said, "Jas, there's plenty of other boys. You deserve better than a greengrocer with a horrible bigger brother."

10:00 P.M.
Oh dear God, Jas on the phone again. Has she done the right thing? etc. etc. etc... I must get her interested in someone else.

Thursday November 19th
8:00 P.M.
Drama drama!!!

We had a substitute teacher today for biology. No, I don't mean substitute, I mean reserve, no, I don't mean that, I mean... oh anyway, a student teacher. She was very nervous and short-sighted and we'd all got that mad bug that you get some days and we couldn't stop laughing. The student teacher, Miss Idris, asked me to hand out pipettes or something and I tried to get up, only to find that Ellen and Jools had tied my Science overall tapes to the drawer handles.

They were helpless with laughter and so couldn't undo them. It took me ages to get free. Then Rosie wrote a note:

This is the plan – Operation Movio Deskio. Whenever Miss Idris writes on the board we all shift our desks back a couple of centimetres, really quietly.

By the end of the lesson when she looked round from the board we were all squashed up against the back wall and there was a three metre gap in front of her. We were speechless with laughing. She just blinked through her glasses and didn't say anything.

Then it happened. Jas and I got to the school gate and Robbie was there. For one moment I thought he had realised that it was ME ME ME he wanted and not old dumbo, but he gave me a HORRIBLE look as I passed by. I said to Jas, "Did you see that? What's he got against me? All right, he's seen my knickers, but it's not a hanging offence."

Jas went a bit red. I said, "Do you know something I don't?"

And she said nervously, in a rush, "Well, erm, maybe. I think he's a bit cross, because Tom's upset we're not going out and I said it was partly because I'd spoken to you and you had said I really shouldn't go out with someone in a fruit and veg shop because it was not really good enough for me. Well, you did say that."

I got hold of her by her tie. "You said *what*????!!!"

She just blinked and went pink and white.

Midnight

I CANNOT BELIEVE IT. Stabbed in the back by my so-called best friend. It was never like this in the Famous Five books. No wonder Robbie is so moody and stroppy with me.

Monday November 23rd
4:15 p.m.

Terrible day. Jackie "suggested" that we do something to pass the time in German, whilst Herr Kamyer amused himself declining verbs on the blackboard. (What a stupid language German is, you have to wait until the end of the sentence to find out what the verb is. But my attitude by then is, Who cares?? I think I might start calling my father Vater and my mum Mutter just for a change. Vati and Mutti, for short.)

Anyway, Jackie said we should mark each other out of ten for physical attractiveness. The list was skin, hair, eyes, nose, figure, mouth, teeth. You had to write out the list and put your name on the top of the paper and then pass it round to everyone to give you a mark. It was Jackie, Alison, Jas, Rosie, Jules, Ellen and Beth Morgan. I didn't want to do it but you don't say no to Jackie. I more or less gave everyone near top marks for everything... even in the face of obvious evidence to the contrary. For instance, I gave Beth seven for her teeth – my logic was that they might be nice when the front ones grow back in, you never know. All the marks were given anonymously. Then we got our papers back with the marks listed.

My list was:

skin	7	8	8	7	8	8	7
hair	8	8	8	8	8	8	8
eyes	7	8	8	8	8	8	8
nose	4	3	3	0	4	4 1/4	4
figure	7	6	7	7	7	7 1/2	7
mouth	6	6	6	6	5	6 1/3	6
teeth	8	8	9	9	8	9	9

Someone gave me a nought for my nose!!! I got the lowest marks out of anyone. My best feature was my teeth! Jas had got mostly eights for all of her features and so she was in that really annoying mood when you've done quite well in an exam and it makes you sort of "kind" to people who haven't done as well. We compared marks on the way home.

"You've got more marks for your mouth than me, Jas. What's wrong with mine? Why is yours so much better? Did you give me six and a third? That looks like your handwriting."

She was squirming a bit by now. "Does it?... No, I don't think it is."

Then I had her. "Well, if it's not that one you must have given me even less than that."

She backed down. "Oh yes, actually, yes, that is my writing, yes."

I was livid. "What is wrong with my mouth?"

"Nothing, that's why I've given you six and a third."

"But that's only average."

"Well, I know I would have given you more, because I think that it's definitely seven or even an eight when it's closed."

"When it's closed," I said dangerously.

Jas was as red as two beetroots. "Well, I had to consider things overall. You see, it's your smile."

"What about my smile?"

"Well when you smile, because your mouth is so big..."

"Yes, do go on..."

"Well, it sort of splits your face in half and it, well, it spreads your nose out more."

7:00 p.m.

In my room in front of the mirror. Practising smiling without making my nose spread. It's impossible. I must never smile again.

8:00 p.m.

Phoned Jas.

"Jas, you only gave me seven and a half for my figure, and I gave you eight for yours."

"Well?"

"Well I only gave you eight because you are my friend."

"Well I only gave you seven and a half because you are my friend. I was going to give you seven."

Midnight

How dare Jas only give me – what was it? – eight for my eyes? I gave her eight for hers and she has got stupid brown eyes.

1:00 a.m.

That stupid Morgan can only have given me four, three or nought for my nose. I gave her six and a half for hers and I was being very bloody generous when I did.

What is the point of being a nice person?

Thursday November 26th

9:00 p.m.

Vati dropped a bombshell today – he is going on a trip to NEW ZEALAND because M and D are thinking of going to live there! I don't know why they bother to tell me. I don't really see what it has to do with me. It was just as I was on the dash to school and Vati said, "Georgia, I don't know if you have heard anything but there's been a lot of redundancies at my place."

I said, "Vati, don't tell me you are going to have to go on the dole with students, and so on. You could always sell your apron if we get too short of money."

Monday November 30th
4:20 p.m.

Jas still moping about Tom. We have to avoid "his" part of town now. I hope I'm not going mad but Rosie told me that she draws stuff on the roof of her mouth with her tongue. Like a heart or a little house. I said she was bonkers but now I've started doing it.

5:00 p.m.

Bumped into the boy up the street I met at Bonfire Night. We sat on our wall for a bit. It's funny, he's one of the only lads I don't feel like I should rush off and cover myself in make-up for. I don't even flick my hair so that it covers half my face (and therefore half my nose). Dad says if I keep doing it I will go blind in one eye, and also that it makes me look like a Pekinese, but what does he know? And anyway, it won't bother him in New Zealand.

Bonfire Boy is called Mark and I suppose the reason I'm not too self-conscious in front of him is that he has a HUGE mouth. I mean it, like Mick Jagger. He is about seventeen and he goes to Parkway, the rough school. He's mad about football and he and his mates go play on the park. I think

I've seen them when I've "accidentally" taken Angus for a walk up there. He's sort of quite attractive (Mark, not Angus), despite the mouth. He wants to be a footballer and has got a trial somewhere. When I left he said, "See you later." Oh no, here we go again, on the "See you later" trail.

9:00 p.m.
Saw Mark walking down the street with his mates. He looked round and up at my bedroom window so I had to bob down quickly. I hope he didn't see me because I had an avocado mask on and my hair Sellotaped down to keep my fringe straight. I wonder where he is going? He had trainers and joggerbums on.

10:30 p.m.
Heard Mutti and Vati arguing. Oh perfect, now they'll split up and they'll both want custody of me.

10:40 p.m.
If I go with Mum I will have access to make-up, clothes, and so on, and I can usually persuade her to let me stay out later.

She laughs at my jokes and goes out a lot. On the other hand, there is Vati.

10:42 p.m.
Ah well, bye bye, Vati...

The Stiff Dylans gig

Tuesday December 1st

11:00 a.m.

Mucho excitemondo! There is going to be a Christmas dance at Foxwood school. Slim announced it in assembly.

"Girls, there is to be a dance at Foxwood school, to celebrate Christmas, on December 12th, commencing at seven thirty."

It was like something out of *Four at Mallory Towers*. Me and Rosie and Jas and Ellen went "Oooohhhhhhhhhhhhhhh ooohhhhhhh!" for so long that Slim had to say "Settle, girls". At last she went on, "To add to the festivities there will be a... band." We started doing our "ooohhhing" again but Hawkeye glared at us so viciously we stopped.

I had thought of shouting "Three cheers for the Headmaster of Foxwood, and three for Merry England!" but I didn't.

Slim still hadn't finished. "The band will be The Stiff Dylans."

Lunchtime
12:30 p.m.
Jas and me had a confab by the vending machine. Jas said, "Do you think we should go? I mean, Lindsay will be there, and Tom might... well, he might go with someone else and then we'd be like..."

"Two spare wotsits at a wedding?" I suggested.

4:00 p.m.
The most cringe-making thing in the Universe of Cringe-making Things happened this afternoon in RE. It was with Miss Wilson, who is not what you might call normal (still, who would be – teaching RE?). She is a very unfortunate person, with ginger hair in a sad bob, her tights are always wrinkly, plus she wears tragic cardigans, usually done up the wrong way. She is not blessed in the looks department, but worse than this, she has not got a personality – at all – none.

Mostly she just talks and we get on with writing notes to each other or filing our nails. Last summer Rosie was so relaxed that she started moisturising her legs during RE. It was so hot that we hadn't been wearing stockings and Rosie put her legs on the desk and started putting cream on them. Well, even Miss Wilson noticed that. I remember she said, "Rosie, you'd better buck up your ideas and buck them up fast." Which struck us as very funny indeed – we were still laughing hours later.

Anyway, this afternoon, for some reason, Miss Wilson got talking about personal hygiene. I swear I don't know how she got there from religious education, maybe people in ancient Hebrew times cast someone out for being a smelly leper. I don't know.

We just heard her say, "Yes, girls, I know how that person felt because when I was younger I had a BO problem myself and people used to avoid me. I never used to wash because I was an orphan and depressed... We just sat there staring at our desks whilst she went on and on about her body odour... it was AWFUL. I have never been so glad to get up and go to PE.

We all ran screaming into the showers and washed ourselves like loonies. Miss Stamp was amazed, she usually has to prod us and shout at us to get us to change at all in winter. She came and looked at us in the shower in amazement. Then we remembered she is a lesbian. So we ran screaming out of the shower.

It's a bloody nightmare of pervs, this school. You'd be safer in Borstal.

8:00 p.m.

Jas came over for the night. We yattered on about a plan for the school dance.

9:00 p.m.

Looking through my bedroom window to see if we could see into next door's bedroom window because I wanted to know what Mr Next Door wore to bed. Jas thought jimjams but I thought shortie nightshirt.

Then as we were looking we saw Mark (Bonfire Boy) coming up the street with a girl. They stopped under a lamppost but I couldn't see what she looked like as they were kissing. Not in the shadows or anything, but under the lamp. We couldn't stop watching and to get a better view we got up on to the window ledge. It was a tight squeeze but you could see everything. Then I heard tip tap tip tap and

Libby came in, carrying her blanket (or blankin' as she calls it – it's not actually a blanket, it's an old bra of Mum's but she likes it and won't let it go. It must have been white once but now it's a horrible grey colour).

She spotted us on the window ledge and said, "Libby see."

I said, "No, Libby, I'm coming down," but then she started saying, "No, no, bad boy, bad boy... me see," and hitting me with her blankin' so that I had to lift her up. Honestly, I'm bullied by a three-year-old and a Scottish wildcat.

I lifted her up and she snuggled down in between me and Jas. She spotted the couple under the lamppost. "Oohh, look! Manlady manlady!!! Hahahaha." It was a bit difficult knowing where Mark ended and the girl began but all was revealed when Mark stopped kissing and looked over her shoulder. Right up at my window. I don't know if he could see us in the dark but we got down from the window ledge so quickly we fell on to my bed. Libby said, "More bouncy now!!!"

Pray God Mark didn't see us spying.

Wednesday December 2nd

8:30 a.m.

Dashing out of the house, Jas and I almost fell into Mark, waiting by the corner. Jas (big pal) said she had to run to her house first and she would see me at school. I went a bit red and walked on with him walking beside me. He said, "Have you got a boyfriend?"

I was speechless. What is the right answer to that question? I tell you what the right answer is... a lie, that's the right answer. So I said, "I've just come out of a heavy thing and I'm giving myself a bit of space."

He looked at me. He really did have the biggest gob I have ever seen. "So is that no?"

And I just stood there and then this really weird thing happened... he touched my breast!!! I don't mean he ripped my blouse off, he just rested his hand on the front of my breast. Just for a second, before he turned and went off to school.

12:30 p.m.

What does it mean when a boy rests his hand on your breast? Does it mean he has the mega-horn? Or was his hand just tired?

4:30 p.m.

Why am I even thinking about this? No sign of Mark (the breast molester) when I got home, thank goodness.

4:45 p.m.

Still, you would think if a boy rests his hand on your breast he might bother to see you sometime.

5:00 p.m.

Up in my bedroom "doing my homework" when the doorbell rang. I put down my magazine and answered it. It was Mark. He said, "I've dumped Ella, do you want to go to The Stiff Dylans gig?"

I said, "Er, well, er, yes thanks."

He said, "OK, see you later."

6:00 p.m.

On the phone to Jas, telling her about Mark, I said, "So then I said, 'Er, yes,' and he said, 'OK, see you later.'"

Jas said, "See you later – what does that mean?"

I said, "I don't know – who does know?... See me later tonight, or at the gig, or what?"

Jas said, "Well, do you like him?"

I thought about it. "I don't really know. He makes me feel like a cobra, you know, all sort of funny and paralysed when the bloke starts playing the bugle thing."

Jas said, "What do you mean? Your head starts bobbing around when he plays his instrument?"

I said, "Don't start, Jas. Anyway, what do you think of him?"

Jas thought. "He's got a very big mouth."

I said, "Yes, I know," and then she said, "But then so have you."

Midnight

Oh-oh. What to do. Why is life so complicated? Do I like Mark? Why did I say yes? Why can't Robbie realise that Lindsay is a drippy git? Ohhhhhhh. *Quel dommage!!! Merde.* Poo.

Monday December 7th
5:00 p.m.

Mark sent a note, which is quite sweet, except that it is very badly written:

Dear Georgia,

Away training till Saturday. Meet you at 8 at clock tower on Saturday.

Mark.

That's it, then. I have no choice. I have to go with him.

9:00 p.m.

Mum comes into my room and says will I come down for a "talk"? I pray it's nothing to do with personal hygiene or her and Dad's relationship problems. Dad seems a bit nervous and he's growing a moustache, how ridiculous, it looks like some small animal is just having a bit of a sleep on his top lip. He says, "Look, Georgie, you're a young woman now (what was I before? a young horse?) and I don't think there should be any secrets in our house (on the contrary, Vati, you will never know about the hand on the breast scenario even if hell freezes over), which is why I need to tell you that as work is so hard to find here in England I am flying off to Auckland straight after Christmas. I'll be staying there for a month or two to get a feel for the place and to try a new job opening there. Then, when I get settled, your mum and you and Libbs can come out and see what you think."

I said, "I know what I think of New Zealand, I have seen *Neighbours*."

Mum said, "Well, that's set in Australia."

What is this, a family crisis or a geography test? I went on patiently, "My point is, Mutti and Vati, that it is very far away, I'm not from there, all my friends are here. Or to put it another way: I would rather let Noel Edmonds adopt me than set foot on New Zealand soil."

We argued for ages – even Libby came down and joined in. She had dressed Angus up in her pyjamas and he had a bonnet on and a dummy in. I don't know how she gets away with it; if I went anywhere near him with a bonnet he would have my hand off.

Midnight
So Vati is off to New Zealand. But that still doesn't solve what I am going to be wearing for The Stiff Dylans gig.

Friday December 11th
2:50 p.m.
Christmas fever has set in at school. We all wore silver

antlers in physics this afternoon. Herr Kamyer tried to join in with the joke by saying, "Oh *ja*, jingle bells, jingle bells." It's pathetic really. Also, why are his trousers so short? You can see acres of pale, hairy ankle between his trousers and his plaid socks. (Yes, I did say plaid socks, now that is not just sad, it's double sad.)

8:00 p.m.
Mutti and Vati strangely quiet and nice to each other. I saw Dad put his arms round Mum in the kitchen. Also Libby was singing, "Dingle balls, dingle balls, dingle on the way," and Dad got all sort of wet round the eyes. Honestly, I thought he was going to cry, which would have been horrific. He picked her up and hugged her really hard. Libby was furious, she called him "Bad, big uggy, bad," and stuck her finger in his eye which made him cry properly.

Saturday December 12th
The Stiff Dylans!
7:00 a.m.
Damn, I didn't mean to wake up so early. Still, it gives me lots of time to get ready for tonight. I thought first of all I

would do my yoga, which I haven't been able to fit into my busy schedule.

7:20 a.m.
Now I know why I don't bother with yoga – it's too hard, that's why. When I did "dog pose" I thought I'd never be able to get up again. I'll just have a lie down and relax with an uplifting book for a few minutes.

7:40 a.m.
I'm not reading the *Tibetan Book of Living and Dying* ever again. I'm not going to become a Buddhist if I might come back reincarnated as a stick insect.

7:50 a.m.
Cup of milky coffee and toast, yum yum yum. Mum has got a new *Cosmo*.

8:10 a.m.
Back in bed for a few minutes' read. Hmmm, "What men say and what they mean".

9:30 a.m.

If a boy says "See you later" it might mean, "Leave me alone, it was great while it lasted but I am not ready for anything more serious" or "See you later".

9:40 a.m.

I am going to become a writer for *Cosmo* – you don't have to make any sense at all. Or maybe I'll be a bloke – they don't have to make any sense either.

10:00 a.m.

I am going to wear my short black Lycra dress. Jas has already phoned five times and changed her mind about what to wear each time.

1:00 p.m.

Rosie has asked the foreign exchange guest student who is staying next door to come to The Stiff Dylans. I said, "Are you sure that's a good idea?" and she said, "He's called Sven," and I said, "Well, that's what I mean."

Rosie says he's a "laugh", whatever that means. She said, "He doesn't speak any English but he is very tall."

When I asked where he was from she said, "I don't know. Denmark, I think. He's blond."

Apparently she asked him to go to The Stiff Dylans by pointing at him, pointing at herself and doing a bit of a dance. She's bonkers. We arranged to go to Boots because we needed to have perfume for tonight and we can use the samples whilst we pretend we might buy them.

4:30 p.m.

Back home, covered in Palomo – I hope it wears off a bit as it's making my eyes water. Also, I've got some new lip gloss which is supposed to plump up your lips. I'm not sure that this is such a good idea in my case, especially going with Mark. I wonder if the same rule applies to lips as does to breasts? I mean, if you use them more, I wonder if they get bigger?

5:00 p.m.

If using your lips does make your lips bigger, what on earth has Mark been up to? Am I going to let him kiss me? What does the hand on the breast mean? Do I want him to be my boyfriend? I don't think he's very bright but he might turn out to be a brilliant footballer like Beckham and then I could marry him and be kept in luxury.

5:10 p.m.
But then I'd be in all the papers. I'd have to have my nose done. I would have to be careful not to smile... what if I forgot? What if I got caught by the paparazzi smiling and my nose spreading all over my face... in the *Daily Express*?

5:15 p.m.
I can't marry him, the pressure is just too much. I am losing my own self-esteem whilst he gets all the attention. I'll have to explain to him tonight that it is all over.

6:00 p.m.
I feel a bit sick. I've got a bit of hair that will NOT go right, in a minute I am going to cut it off. Also, I think I have got knobbly knees. Maybe when I am Mark's wife I could have fat injected into them (possibly taken from my nose, so it would be a two-in-one operation... smaller nose and fatter knees all in one swift plunge of the huge, hypodermic, fat-extractor needle... er, I really do feel sick...).

7:30 p.m.

I wish I had gone with Jas and Rosie, all in a big gang. Now it means I'll have to walk in with Mark and everyone will look at me and think he's my boyfriend.

Midnight

I cannot BELIEVE my life. Well, if you could call it a life... When I think about tonight I feel like staying in bed for the rest of it.

Mark was at the clock tower, smoking a fag... he looked sort of OK. When I got near him he grabbed me and gave me a kiss right on the mouth, no messing about. I was surprised and also a bit worried... maybe the hand would sneak up to the breast for a bit of a rest... but no.

Mark doesn't seem to say much – after the kiss he took my hand and we started walking to the gig. It was a bit awkward because I am actually bigger than him, so I had to sort of let my shoulder down on one side like Quasimodo.

As soon as we got there Mark went to say hello to a few of his mates. Rosie's Sven was a GIANT – about eight foot tall, with a crewcut. Jas was all moony and looked a bit pale.

She said, "I wanted that anorexic model look, like I've been up partying all night. I want Tom to think I've not been thinking about him."

The gig was packed, mostly boys on one side and girls on the other. Jas said, "Aren't you going to talk to your boyfriend?"

Which is when Tom and Robbie walked in. They saw us and Robbie caught my eye and he smiled... I'd forgotten what a Sex God he is. He's all muscly and dark and oohhhhh. I smiled back, a proper smile because I'd forgotten about my nose for the moment. Then from behind me came Lindsay and crossed over to Robbie. He had been smiling at her!!! My face was so red you could fry an egg on it. Robbie kissed Lindsay on the cheek. She had her hair up and was quite literally all ears. Yukko.

Robbie went up on stage and Tom was left by himself as wet Lindsay chatted to some of her stupid, sixth-form mates. Jas said, "Do you think I should go over and say something to him?"

I said, "Have some pride, Jas, he chose vegetables over you." At that moment a dark-haired girl came out of the loos and went over to Tom. She put her hand on his arm and they went off together.

And it got worse.

The Stiff Dylans started playing and Mark came across to me, got hold of my hand and pulled me on to the dance floor. His Mick Jagger impersonation did not stop at the lips. He was a lunatic on the dance floor, strutting around with his hands on his hips. I nearly died. Then Sven joined in, dragging Rosie with him. His style of dancing was more Cossack, a lot of going down into a squat position and kicking his legs out. Then he lifted Rosie up above his head!!! He was whirling her around, going, "Oh *ja*, oh *ja*," and Rosie was trying to keep people from seeing up her skirt.

And that is when I lost it. It was just too funny... Jas, Ellen and Jools and I were laughing like hyenas. I had a coughing fit and had to rush to the loos to try and recover. I'd just calm myself down and then poke my head round the door to see Sven dancing around and it started me off again.

Then Mark wanted to slow dance. I knew because he grabbed me and pulled me up against him. He was all lumpy, if you know what I mean, and had his mouth against my neck. It was even more difficult dancing with him than it was holding hands. I had to sort of bend my knees and sag a bit in order to "fit in". At one stage I found myself looking straight at Robbie. He looked so cool. Oh bloody *sacré bleu*. Even though I hate him and he is a pompous pratboy, I think I may love him.

Then the band stopped playing for a break but Mark yelled, "Play more." Some of his mates started joining in, then they sort of rushed the stage and Mark grabbed the microphone from Robbie. He was "singing" – I think it may have been "Jumpin' Jack Flash". Robbie put his hand on his shoulder and then a massive fight broke out. All Mark's thick friends got stuck into the band and then the band's mates got stuck into them. All us girls were screaming.

Sven lifted two boys up at once and tossed them outside into the street and that's when Ellen, Jas, Jools and I decided to do a runner.

So, a gorgeous night. I am tucked up in bed, my "boyfriend" is a hooligan, before him I had another "boyfriend" called whelk boy. The boy I like hates me and prefers a wet weed with sticky-out ears...

ps My so-called 'pet' spat at me when I walked in all upset.

pps I have found my sister's secret used nappy at the bottom of my bed.

Sunday December 13th

5:00 p.m.

No sign of Mark, thank goodness. I stayed in reading all day. Mum and Dad are having a night out – they suddenly want to do things together, it's so unnatural! – so I have to babysit Libby. I don't mind as I never want to go out again.

6:00 p.m.

Libby cheered me up by pretending to be Angus. She curled up in his basket and hid behind the curtains, growling. I had to stop her when she started eating his dinner.

6:15 p.m.

Jas on the phone. "I'll never get a boyfriend. I may become a vet."

6:20 p.m.

Jas phoned again. "Do you think I am really ugly?"

6:30 p.m.

Rosie phoned. "I managed to get Sven home before the

police arrived. He has given me a bit of holly."

I said, "Why?" and she said, "I don't know, maybe it's a Danish tradition."

7:15 p.m.
Jools phoned. "Someone said they noticed that Lindsay wears an engagement ring when she's at school."

8:00 p.m.
Perfect. The doorbell rang but I made Libby be really quiet and pretend we weren't in. No note or anything.

Fed up, depressed, hungry.

9:00 p.m.
Fed up, depressed, feel sick.

Had:

2 Mars bars,

toast,

milky coffee,

Ribena,

Coke,

toast,

cornflakes and
Pop-Tarts.

10:00 p.m.
Going to bed. Hope I never wake up.

Monday December 14th
8:30 a.m.
Nearly bumped into Mark on the way to school. Got round the corner just in time, thank goodness.

9:45 a.m.
Slim was livid about The Stiff Dylans gig; she was trembling like a loon.

"I sincerely hope none of my girls were in any way associated with the hooligans who behaved like animals at the dance..."

Rosie looked up at me and put her teeth in front of her bottom lip like a hamster. I don't know why but it really made me laugh so much I thought I would choke. I had to pretend to have a coughing fit and get my hankie out.

Jas wasn't in school. I wonder where she is. Maybe the

"painters are in", if you know what I mean. Rosie was full of Sven this and Sven that. I said, "Is he your boyfriend, then?" and she went a bit red and said, "Look, I don't think we're going out or anything. He's only given me a bit of holly." But as I said, that could mean anything in Denmark.

Oh bloody hell, Jackie and Alison, the Bummer twins, are back with a vengeance. They sent a note round saying they want us all to meet by the canteen on Thursday lunch for, as they call it, "the latest".

4:30 p.m.

Note from Mark when I got in from school: *Georgia, I looked for you after the other night. Meet me at 10 at the phone box tonight. Mark*

9:50 p.m.

If I don't go I'll only see him in the street anyway...

I shouted to M and D (spending time together AGAIN), "I'm just taking Angus out for a walk."

Dad yelled, "Don't let him near that poodle."

I had to drag Angus away from Next Door's, he wants to eat that poodle. He has about four cans of petfood a day as it is. If he gets any bigger Mum says she is going to give him to a zoo, as if they would want him.

10:00 p.m.

Mark smoking by the phone box. He didn't see me coming – hardly surprising as Angus had dragged me behind a hedge, chasing a cat. In the end I tied him to the gatepost. From behind the hedge I could see Mark, and you know when you have one of those moments when you know what you have to do? No, well neither do I... but I did think, I must come clean with Mark, it is not fair on him, I'm going to say, "Look, Mark, I like you and you mustn't think it's you, it's me really, I just think I could never make you happy, we're so different. I think it is best that we stop right here and now before anyone gets hurt."

So I went up to him. He was half in the shadows and he threw his cigarette down when he saw me. I opened my mouth to speak and he just kissed me right on the open mouth. What if I had been sucking a Polo mint? I could have choked to death!! Also, he put his tongue in my mouth, which was a bit of a surprise... but then he did it again!!! He put his hand on my breast! What was I supposed to do? I hadn't gone to breast classes. My arms were sort of hanging by my sides like an orang-utan when I remembered what whelk boy had said about putting your hands on someone's waist, so I did that. He had one hand on my breast and one on my bottom. But just when I was thinking, What next? in the hand department, he stopped kissing me.

Was this a good moment to say he was dumped?

He said, "Look, Georgia, this is not personal or anything, but er... I think you are too young for me. I'm going back out with Ella because she lets me do things to her. Sorry, see you later."

Midnight

See you later? Mark has had the cheek to dump me just as I was about to dump him! I'm never getting up again. Ella lets him do things to her... what things? Two hands on her breasts?

Wednesday December 16th
1:30 p.m.

Jas still not back. I'll visit her after school.

4:15 p.m.

No reply at Jas's house.

6:30 p.m.

Phoned Jas. Her mum said she couldn't get to the phone as she is not very well. I said, "Is it the flu?" and her mum said, "Well, I don't know, but she's not eating."

Not eating. Jas. Jas not eating. Things are bad. I said, "What, not even Pop-Tarts?" and her mum said, "No."

Things are much worse than I thought.

Thursday December 17th

10:00 a.m.

Still no Jas. This is getting ridiculous.

1:30 p.m.

Jackie and Alison's "latest thing" turns out to be so bonkers it is not even in the bonkers universe. We all had to go out into the freezing cold at the back of the tennis courts... I was surprised that Jackie knew where they were. I don't think she's ever been near the sports area before. Then Jackie told us what it was all about. "OK, this is what you do. You crouch down like this, then you start panting really hard and then you stand up and start running forward."

I said, "Why?" and she looked at me and lit a fag. Tarty or what? She had a huge spot on her chin, it looked like a second nose. I'm not surprised her skin is so bad, it's probably been covered in make-up since she was five.

She blew the smoke in my face and said, "When you run forward it makes you faint."

Even Rosie, who usually doesn't say much to Jackie, had to repeat this, "You faint?"

Jackie drew on her fag like she was dealing with the very, very stupid. She didn't say anything, so eventually Rosie said, "Then what?"

Jackie totally lost it, then. "Look, four-eyes, think about how useful it can be to just faint when you want to... in assembly – faint, get taken out. In physics, when you haven't done your homework – faint, get taken out... games... anything."

Rosie is nothing if not stupid, so she kept going on. "Don't you think someone might notice if we crouched down in assembly or physics and started panting and then ran forward?"

Jackie walked over to Rosie, and she is quite a big girl. Her breasts are sturdy-looking and she's got big arms.

11:00 p.m.

I still feel a bit odd. I'm not going to be doing anything that Jackie and Alison say ever again. That is it. This stupid fainting thing is it. That is it. I did the panting and then stood up and started running and I did feel very faint, but not as faint as when I ran into Mr Attwood coming out of his hut. I may have broken my shin. Sadly Elvis was OK.

Friday December 18th
7:30 p.m.

Jas off all week. I'm worried about her now, she won't even speak to me on the phone. Even when I pretended I was Santa Claus.

Friday December 25th
10:00 a.m.

Happy St Nicholas's Day, one and all!!!

My fun-filled day started at five fifteen a.m. when Libby came in to give me my present, something made out of

Playdough that had horrible, suspicious-looking brown bits in it. She said, "Tosser's baby... ahhh," and tucked it up into bed with me.

As we are "a bit strapped for cash" as Vati puts it (due to his inability to hold down a job in my opinion, but I didn't say in case I spoiled Christmas even more) we could not have expensive presents. Mum and Dad got me CDs and make-up and leggings and trainers and undies and perfume, and I made Dad a lovely moustache holder which I think he will treasure.

I made Mum some homemade cosmetics out of egg yolks and stuff. She tried on the face pack and it gave her a bit of a rash, but on the whole livened up her complexion.

I made Libby a fairy costume, which was a big mistake as she spent the rest of the day changing us into things by whacking us with her wand. I had to be a "nice porky piggy" for about an hour. I never want to see a sausage again.

Jas phoned, but still isn't venturing out – so no escaping "merry" Christmas with the family.

Angus looked nice in his tinsel crown until it annoyed him and he ate it. When we had our lunch Mum made him a special mouse-shaped lunch in his bowl out of Katto-meat.

He ate its head and then sat in it. Heaven knows what goes on in his cat brain.

I think I may become a New Age person next year and celebrate the winter solstice by leaving my family and going to Stonehenge to dance with Druids. It couldn't be more boring than watching my dad trying to make his new electric toothbrush work. However, there was a bright moment when he got it tangled up in his moustache.

Saturday December 26th
Noon

Quel dommage!! M and D have selfishly asked me to babysit Libby whilst they have "a last night out together". Dad leaves for Whangamata on the 29th... sob, sob... and so as a brilliant treat he is taking Mum... to the pub!! With Uncle Eddie!!

If I was Mum I would have faked an accident, or if necessary had a real accident. A broken ankle would be a small price to pay to avoid Uncle Eddie's version of "Agadoo".

11:30 p.m.
Mum and Dad came crashing in, giggling. They were drunk. I was in bed TRYING to sleep but they have no consideration. I could hear them dancing around to "The Birdy Song". They are sad.

Then they crept upstairs saying "Ssshhhh" really loudly. Mum gave a bit of a gasp when she came into my room because Libby was in bed with me but she had gone to sleep upside down so her feet were on the pillow next to me. Mum put her in her own bed, but then horror of horrors DAD RUFFLED MY HAIR. I pretended even harder to be asleep.

Sunday December 27th

11:00 a.m.
M and D still in bed. I will take their lovely young daughter Liberty in to them to chat.

2:00 p.m.
Going out. Dad's given me a fiver to look after Libby.

Tuesday December 29th
8:00 p.m.

Vati left today. I must say even I had a bit of a cry. He went off in Uncle Eddie's sidecar. We all waved him off. He says that he'll ring when he gets to Whangamata. It takes two days to fly there – imagine that. I suppose it is the other side of the world. Mum is all glum and snivelling, so I bought her some Milk Tray. That made her cry more, so I don't think I'll do it again. Libby got her Angus's bowl to cry into.

Exploding Knickers

Friday January 1st

11:00 a.m.

Resolutions:

I will be a much nicer person, to people who deserve it.

I will be interested in my future.

I will speak nicely to Mr and Mrs Next Door.

I will be less superficial and vain.

I will concentrate on my positive and not my negative, e.g. I will think less about my nose and more about my quite attractive teeth.

Saturday January 2nd

11:30 a.m.

At last! News of Jas. It seems that she might have glandular fever. I'm wearing a scarf over my mouth and nose when I visit her, just in case. Apparently you get glandular fever from kissing. It's a nightmare, this kissing business – if it's not a mysterious hand on the breast it's huge swollen glands. Celibacy or a huge fat neck, that is the stark choice. I wonder if Slim has got big fat feet from too much kissing in the foot area? Uuurgghh, now I feel really sick. I'm far too ill to visit the sick. I must go home to bed.

No... Jas needs me. I'll just try not to breathe the same air as her.

4:00 p.m.

Jas has finally let me see her. She's all pale and thin, just lying in bed. Her bedroom is tidy, which is a bad sign and she has turned her mirror to the wall. She didn't even open her eyes when I came in. I sat on her bed.

"Jas, what are you doing? What's the matter? Come on, tell me, your best pal."

Silence.

"Come on, Jas, whatever it is, you can trust me."

Silence.

"I know what it is, you think that just because everyone else besides Nauseating P. Green and Hairy Kate the lezzo have got boyfriends – or have kissed someone properly –

145

there is something really wrong with you, don't you?"

Silence. I was getting a bit irritated. I was trying to help and I had problems of my own. I was practically an orphan, for instance... and a substitute parent. It was all, "Will you babysit Libby?" since Dad had selfishly gone to the other side of the world. What did Jas know of trouble? Had she taken her little sister to the swimming pool? No, she didn't even have a little sister. Had her little sister's swimming knickers exploded at the top of the toddlers' water slide? No. Is there ever any point in trying to tell Mum that Libby always has bottom trouble after baked beans? No, there is not. The swimming knickers could not contain Libby's poo explosion and it was all over the slide and nearby toddlers. Did Jas know what it was to see a pool being cleared of sobbing toddlers, dragged out by their water wings? No. Did she know what it was like to sluice her little sister down and then have to walk the gamut of shame past all the mothers and toddlers and swimming-pool attendants in masks with scrubbing brushes? I think not. I had to take it on the chin like a taking-it-on-the-chin person, so why couldn't Jas?

I didn't say any of this to Jas but I took a tough line.

"Come on, Jas, what can be so bad about swollen-up glands?"

Jas spoke in a quiet voice so I had to bend down to hear her. "I haven't got swollen-up glands. I don't think I'll ever get a boyfriend, no one asked me to dance even. Tom was my only chance and even he preferred his onions."

Aha, time for all that stuff I read in Mum's *Feel the Fear and Do it Anyway* book. I got Jas's mirror from the wall and held it in front of her face. "Look into that mirror, Jas, and love the person that you see. Say, I love you."

Jas looked in the mirror – she couldn't help it, it was about three centimetres away from her nose. She was almost sick. "Uuurggghhhh, I look hideous."

She wasn't really getting it. I said, "Jas, Jas, love yourself, love the beauty that is there, look at that lovely face, look at that lovely mouth. The mouth that your friend marked eight out of ten. Think of that, Jas. Think of all the poor people who only got six and a third... and you have an eight for a mouth..." (I can be like an elephant for remembering things that annoy me. Sadly I can remember nothing to do with French, history, maths or biology.)

Jas was definitely perking up. She was puckering her

mouth and trying for a half-smile. "Do you really think I have got a nice mouth?"

"Yes, yes, but look at the rest of you, look at those eyes, look at the spot-free skin..."

Jas sat up. "I know, it's good, isn't it? I've been drinking lemon and hot water first thing."

Monday January 4th
7:00 a.m.
Woke up and felt happy for a minute until I realised I had to go back to loony headquarters (school) today.

2:30 p.m.
Gym. Discovered Angus had stored his afternoon snack in my rucksack. There are hedgehog quills in my sports knickers.

Tuesday January 12th
Noon
Victory. Victory.

Madame Slack has been on my case about being lazy in French and I have just got eighty-five per cent in a test. Hahahaha. *Fermez la bouche*, Madame Slack. I did it by learning twenty-five words and then making sure I answered every question by using only those words. So to question one – "In French, what is your favourite food?" my answer was "*Lapin*" (rabbit).

For my essay, "What did you do on a sunny day?" I made sure I played with a rabbit.

Describe a favourite book – *Watership Down* – lots of *lapins* in that.

1:00 p.m.

In line with my new resolution to concentrate on school and not boys I went to do my yoga in the gym at lunchtime. My yoga routine is called The Sun Salute and you stretch up to welcome the sun and then you bend down as if to say "I am not worthy." Then you do cobra pose and dog pose... it's all very flowing and soothing.

1:15 p.m.

Miss Stamp came in just as I was doing dog post. She said, "Oh, don't let me disturb you. I'm glad you're taking an interest in yoga, it's one of the best exercises for the body. It will be really good for your tennis in summer. Don't mind me, I'm just getting ready for this afternoon." Well, I was upside down with my bottom sticking up in the air. Not something you want to do in front of a lesbian. So I quickly went into cobra but that made it look like I was sticking my breasts out at her. I think she may now be growing a beard as well as a moustache.

Honestly, there is no bloody peace in this place.

1:30 p.m.

I tried my yoga outside, even though it was hard to do it with my gloves and coat on. Again I'd just got into dog pose when Elvis appeared round the corner. He's a grumpy old nutcase. "What are you up to?" he shouted at me.

I said, from upside down, "Nnn doing nmy nyoga."

He pulled down his cap. "I don't care if you're doing nuclear physics, you're not doing it in my yard. Clear off before I report you."

As I went, I said, "Did you know that Elvis is dead?"

4:30 p.m.

Saw Mark on my way home. I smiled in a mature way at him. He just said, "All right?"

4:30 p.m.

Walking home with Jas. I think she is well on the way to recovery. "What do you think of this lip gloss? Do you think it makes me look a bit like Claudia Schiffer? My mouth is the same shape, I think." I wish I hadn't started this. Still, if she wants to live in a fantasy wonderland and it cheers her up... We went to her house and up to her room. Oh, the bliss of a normal household, no mad mum, no strange sister, no wild animals. Jas's mum asked us if we would like some Ribena and sandwiches. Imagine my mum doing that?... Imagine my mum being in! I suppose she is a good role model... if you want to be a hospital administrator – but couldn't she make the odd sandwich as well?

In Jas's bedroom we did our vital statistics with her tape measure. I am thirty-two, twenty-three, thirty-two and Jas is thirty, twenty-three, thirty-three. I think she was breathing in for the twenty-three myself. Also my legs are two inches longer than hers. (I didn't mention it to Jas but one of my legs is two inches longer and the other one is only one and a half inches longer. How can you develop a limp at my age? It might be because I carry my bag on one shoulder and it's making that side longer. I must remember to swap sides. Nobody likes a lopsided girl.)

Thursday January 28th
3:30 p.m.

Rosie got up first and left the room. Miss Wilson came in as we were working, to "supervise", but we asked her who invented God and she left pretty quickly. We were busy making a list of all the qualities we want in a boyfriend – sense of humour, good dancer, good kisser, nice smile, six-pack, etc. Rosie sent her list and it just said, *HUGE*. I wrote back, Huge teeth, you mean? And she replied, *Yes*. Sven has begun to infect her with his Danishness, I think.

Anyway, Rosie, Jools and Ellen went out first, and then me and Jas. We met up in the ground floor loos and put our boots and skinny tops and make-up on. We made sure the coast was clear and then went out of the back doors. We had to crouch down beneath the science-block windows – Hawkeye was teaching in there and she could smell a girl at twenty paces. Once past the Science block it was a quick dash behind Elvis's hut. He was in there, reading his newspaper, and as we crept by we heard him fart loudly and

♡ 153

say "Pardon". I started giggling and then everyone caught it. We had to run like mad. All afternoon if anyone did anything we'd say "Pardon".

Great in Boots. We tried all the testers, and this stuff that you put on your hair, like a wand and it puts a streak of colour into your own hair. I tried all of them but blonde looked really brilliant. Just a streak across the front, I knew it would look good. I'm going to get Mum to let me dye my hair blonde now that Vati's safely in Whangamata.

Midnight
Brilliant day!!! Jas and I sung "Respect" by Aretha Franklin on the way home.

Jas must die

Saturday February 6th
11:00 a.m.

The doorbell rang. Mum was in the loo debagging Libby; it was not a pretty sight. At the weekend Mum wears these awful dungarees that only lesbians or people on *Blue Peter* in the sixties wear. Libby was singing "Three bag bears, three bag bears, see how they run, see how they run…" ("Three Blind Mice" to other people). Libby was as happy as a mad sandbag but Mum was all flustered. "Will you answer that, Georgie? It will be this builder called Jem I phoned up to look at the lounge. Let him in and make a cup of coffee while I finish with this."

When I opened the door I got an impression of blond hair and denims but then there was this awful squealing from next door's garden. Mrs Next Door was screeching,

"Get him, get him! Oh oh oh!" She was dashing around the garden with a broom. I thought that Angus had got the poodle at last, but when I looked over the fence he had a little brown thing in his mouth.

Mrs Next Door yelled at me, "I'm going to call the police! It's my niece's guinea pig, we're looking after it. And now this, this... THING has got it."

Angus crouched down not very far away. I said, in my sternest voice, "Drop it, now drop it, Angus."

Due to my training he recognised my voice and let the guinea pig drop out of his mouth. I started to go over to get it and the guinea pig started scampering away. After it had got a few centimetres Angus put his huge paw out and just let it rest on the end of its bottom. It squiggled and squiggled and Angus yawned and took his paw off again. The guinea pig streaked off and Angus lumbered to his feet and ambled after it. He biffed it on to its back and then he sat on it and closed his eyes for a little doze. I said to Mrs Next Door, "Sorry, he can be very annoying, he's having a game with it." She was very unreasonable. I managed to lure Angus away from his little playmate with a kipper. Mrs ND says she is going to complain to someone official. I wonder who? Cat patrol, I suppose.

Jem had been watching from the doorstep. He had a nice, crinkly smile. He said, "He's big for a cat, isn't he?"

I sighed, "Come in, Mum's in the bathroom, she'll be out in a minute." Jem came into the front room and I gave him some of my coffee. He's quite good-looking for an older man.

Mum came rushing in in her dungarees. Then she saw Jem and went all weird and even redder. She said, "Nnnnghhhh!" and then just left the room.

I shrugged my shoulders at Jem. He said, "Are you doing your GCSEs?" (Good, he thought I was at least sixteen... hahahahaha)... I went "Nnngghhh" as well. Then Mum came back with LIPSTICK on and proper clothes. I left them to it.

Sunday February 7th
11:00 a.m.

Got dressed in a short skirt, then me and Jas walked up and down to the main road. We wanted to see how many cars with boys in them hooted at us. Ten!! (We had to walk up and down for four hours... still, ten is ten!!!)

Monday February 22nd
4:15 p.m.

Something really odd happened today when Jas and I left school. Robbie was at the school gate in his mini. He was leaning against it. I wish my legs didn't go all jelloid when I see him. How do you make yourself not like someone? I think you're supposed to concentrate on some of their bad points. Maybe he's got horrible hands? I looked at his hands... they are lovely – all strong-looking but quite artistic too. Like he could put up a shelf and also take you to a plateau of sensual pleasure at the same time. I bet he doesn't rest his hand on your breast... I wish he would. Shut up!!!!! Anyway, I was getting ready to put on my coolest look and he said, "Hello, Jas, how are you?"

Jas flushed and said, "Oh, hi, Robbie, yeah fine thanks, and you?"

He said, "Cool." Then he said, "Jas, could I have a... could I speak to you sometime? Maybe you would come for a coffee next Wednesday after school?"

And Jas went, "Er... well...er... yes. Fine. See you then."

I was quite literally speechless.

When we got to Jas's house I just walked in through the

gate, through the door and straight up the stairs into her bedroom. It was like I had a furball in my throat. I thought I was going to choke and explode and poo myself all at the same time.

Jas sat down on her bed and just went "Foof".

I said, "What do you mean by 'Foof'?"

And she said, "Just that... 'Foof'."

I said, "Well, what does he want to see you about?"

And she looked at her nails in a very annoying way. "I don't know."

I said, "Well, you won't go, will you?"

And she said, "He asked me to go for a coffee and I said I would."

I went on, "Yes, but you won't go, will you?"

She looked at me, "Why shouldn't I go? He said he wanted to talk to me."

I couldn't believe it. "But you know he's my sworn enemy."

Jas went all reasonable. "Yes, but he's not my sworn enemy, he seems to really like me."

I was beyond the Valley of the Livid. "Jas, if you are my friend you will not go and meet Robbie."

She just went silent and tight-lipped. I slammed out of her house.

Tuesday February 23rd
11:00 p.m.

I left the house ten minutes early today and walked on the other side of the road. Jas usually hangs about outside her gate between eight thirty-five and eight forty-five and then she walks on if I don't turn up. I ran like mad past her house, keeping to cover, and arrived ten minutes before assembly.

Hawkeye stopped me. "I've never seen you early for anything, what's going on? I'll be keeping my eye on you." Honestly, she's so suspicious. I don't suppose she's got anything else to do, no real life of her own. When I went into the assembly hall I didn't stand in my usual place, I went and talked to Rosie. Jas came in to where we stand together, she caught my eye and gave a half-smile but I gave her my worst look.

I didn't see her again until lunch when she came into the loos. I was sort of trapped because I was drying my fringe under the hand dryer. I'd slept on it funny and it was all sticking up. My head was upside down and she said, "Look, this is really silly, we can't fall out over some bloke."

I said, "Nyot snum bluk."

She said, "Pardon?"

I stood up and faced her. "Jas, you know what I've been through with Robbie, he is not just 'some bloke'."

She was being Mrs Reasonable Knickers. "What are you so bothered about? It's just coffee... at the moment."

I pounced on that like a rat on a biscuit. "What do you mean, 'at the moment'?"

She was putting chapstick on, pouting in the mirror... she really has snapped, she thinks she looks like Claudia Schiffer. "I'm just saying, it's only coffee at the moment, if anything else happens of course I will let you know first." That's when I kicked her on the shin. HOW DARE SHE? That is it!!! I'm never speaking to her again.

Saturday February 27th
10:00 a.m.

Mum up and humming in the kitchen like a happy person, whatever that is. I've made a list of my friends:

I have 12 "close casuals",

20 "social only" and

6 "inner circle" (you know, the kind of friends who would cry properly at your funeral).

Libby is too small to be a chum, although she's a better chum than some, if you know what I mean. Jas is not on my list.

10:30 a.m.
I wonder if I have got enough friends? I worry that if British Telecom asks me for ten friends and family for my list of cheap calls I would have to count the astrological phone line for Librans which I ring more often than not.

11:00 a.m.
Doorbell went. Mum shouted, "Will you get that?" It was Jem; he really is quite cool and fit-looking. He was wearing a T-shirt and you could see his muscly arms. I smiled at him. Maybe I need an older man to teach me the ways of love...

11:05 a.m.
Mum came rushing out of the bedroom with Libbs. "Take Libby for a walk, love, will you? Thanks. Now, Jem, would you like a cup of coffee?"

He said, "I wouldn't say no, I've got a bit of a hangover."

She giggled (yes, she giggled), and said, "Honestly, what are you like? Did you have a good time?"

They went off into the kitchen. He said, "Yeah, we went to this club, it's a laugh, you should come one night."

She giggled and said, "Be careful, I might take you up on that."

I couldn't hear what happened after that because Libby hit me with her monkey. "Out now," she said, so I had to go.

What next? My mum goes off with a builder whilst my vati is trying to build a new life for her in the Antipodes?

Actually, when put like that, it seems fair enough...

Vati sent a letter and some photos from Whangamata. In his letter he said, **The village has the most geothermal activity in the world. When I had lunch in the garden the other day, the table was heaving and lurching around... I could hardly eat my steak. The ground lurches and heaves around because underneath the earth's crust thousands of billions of tons of molten steam is trying to get out. The trees go backwards and forwards, the sheep go up and down...**

Oh, very good, Vati, I'll be over there on the next flight. Not. And he sent some photos of his New Zealand mates... They were all heavily bearded like the Rolf Harris quadruplets.

Still, he is my vati, I will have to have a word with Mum in order to save the family.

12:05 p.m.
Can't be bothered.

My dad has become Rolf Harris

Monday March 1st
10:30 a.m.
Still not speaking to Jas, but things have gone horribly wrong in that she is not speaking to me either. I don't know how this has happened as I was supposed to be in charge. It's bloody difficult coming to school because if she gets ahead of me I have to walk really, really slowly behind her because my legs are longer.

Wednesday March 3rd
9:00 a.m.
Today is the day that Jas is to meet Robbie after school for a "coffee". I wonder if Lindsay knows about this? I wonder if I have a duty to tell her?

3:00 p.m.

I can't help myself – I have been trailing Jas around all day. I notice she has her very short skirt on and she's done her hair. Perhaps I could leap on her as she comes out of the loo and duff her up, or I could pay Jackie and Alison to do it.

3:15 p.m.

Rosie, Ellen and Jools are not taking sides in this, which I hate... how dare they be so fair-minded? Rosie said, "He's only asked her for a coffee to talk... you don't know what about," and Jools said, "It's a free world, you know, you can't make people do anything."

How dim and thick can you be? I'd stop speaking to them but then I wouldn't have anyone to talk to at all.

4:05 p.m.

He's there in his mini!! Where is Lindsay? Perhaps there will be a fight at the gates. There was a fight once before but that was Mr Attwood and an ice-cream man. Elvis had gone to see him off. He went up to the van and said, "Clear off!" and the ice-cream man said, "Make me, short arse."

166

Elvis took off his glasses and his cap and said, "Come out of that van and I will."

So the ice-cream man did come out of his van and he was about twenty-five foot tall and Elvis said, "Right, well, I've told you. That's my final word... As soon as you have sold as many ice creams as you want, you must leave the school boundaries."

4:08 p.m.

No sign of Lindsay. I said to Rosie and Jools and Ellen, "Where is Lindsay?"

And Rosie said, "She's playing badminton." For heaven's sake, she is so wet – some snivelling, scheming snot takes her fiancée/boyfriend and all she can do is run around in sports knickers, hitting a ping-pong ball with some feathers stuck in it.

4:10 p.m.

Jas came out in boots. Suede boots, knee-length, with heels!! She'll get offered money if she hangs around in the streets looking like that.

4:12 p.m.

She has reached the gates. Robbie has opened the door of his mini and gone round the other side and driven off.

Home

4:38 p.m.

I'm going mad. What are they doing now?

5:00 p.m.

Ring Rosie. "Have you heard anything?"

   Rosie: "No."

   I said, "Well, call me if you do."

5:20 p.m.

I've called everyone and nobody has heard anything yet. It's like being in one of those crap plays we have to study. I'll be left lonely and looking out to sea at the end... possibly with a beard.

5:30 p.m.

I've just found I've got hairs growing out of my armpits. How did they get there? They weren't there yesterday.

5:40 p.m.

I've got some on my legs as well. I'd better distract myself by getting rid of them with Mum's razor.

6:00 p.m.

Oh God! Oh God! I'm haemorrhaging. My legs are running with blood – I had to staunch the flow with Mum's dressing-gown. She'll kill me if she finds out. I'd better wash it.

6:10 p.m.

Put it in the washing machine with some other stuff before she gets home.

6:30 p.m.

Phone rings. It's only Mum. She and Libby are round at Uncle Eddie's and won't be home until later and I've got to get my own tea. *Quelle surprise!*

Go to the fridge.

6:32 p.m.

I wonder what I'll have? Hmmm... oh, I know, I'll have this mouldy old tin of beans that is the only thing in there...

7:00 p.m.

Phone rings.

I fell over the cord getting to it, legs started bleeding again. It was Rosie. "Jas just phoned."

I almost screamed at her. "And???"

"Well, they had coffee, she says he really is fantastic-looking and also very funny."

"And?"

"Well, he wanted to talk to her about Tom."

I started laughing. "Hahahahahha... and she wore her boots. Hahaha."

Rosie went on, "Yes, he wanted to know if she still likes Tom because he still likes her."

I put the phone down. Tom. Who cares? Hahahaha.

Life is fabby fab fab fabbity fab fab.

7:30 p.m.

La lalalalalalala. Fabbity fab fab.

7:40 p.m.

Yum yum, beans. Lovely lovely beans.

10:00 p.m.

Oh dear, slight problem. Mum's dressing gown has shrunk to the size of a doll's dressing gown. It might fit Libby, I suppose.

Hmmm.

Still. Fabbity fab fab. I'll think about it tomorrow. For now I must just dance about a bit to a loud tune.

11:00 p.m.

Heard Mum come in but I pretended I was asleep. I've hidden the dressing gown at the bottom of my wardrobe.

Thursday March 4th

8:30 a.m.

Jas was waiting for me at her gate. I saw her and started walking really slowly and pretending to be looking through my bag for something. Then I acted like I'd forgotten something and had to go home for it. I walked back and waited behind a hedge for about four minutes and then walked back again. Hurrah, she was gone, my plan worked. But just as I passed her gate she popped up from behind her hedge. She walked alongside me and didn't say anything and neither did I. It's funny being silent – you have to be careful to not make any noise. You can't belch or anything or even clear your throat in case the other person thinks you are going to speak first. When we got to school she handed me a letter. I wouldn't take it at first but I quite wanted to read it so I did eventually put it in my bag.

1:00 p.m.
First opportunity I've had to read the letter because I didn't want Jas to know that I was keen to read any stupid thing she had to say.

The letter said,

Dear Georgie,

I am sorry that a boy has come between us, it will never happen again. I was stupid and didn't think of your feelings even though you are my best friend. If there is anything I can do to be your friend again, I will do it.

Jas

PS He isn't engaged to Lindsay.

1:15 p.m.

So Jas thinks she can just forget the whole sorry affair – drop it just like that. Well, it will take more than a note to make me change my mind about her.

1:20 p.m.

Jas found me by the vending machine and she was a bit nervous. Let her suffer.

1:21 p.m.

Jas went "Er..." and I said, "What do you mean he's not engaged to Lindsay?"

In my room
5:00 p.m.

Jas is helping me to stretch Mum's dressing gown. As a punishment for her appalling behaviour she has promised that she will say it was her who put it in the washing-machine. My mum won't get cross with Jas.

5:15 p.m.

The dressing gown is exactly the same doll size except that

now it has very long arms like an orang-utan.

5:25 p.m.
Apparently Robbie was very surprised that he was supposed to be engaged. When he asked Jas why she thought that, she had to pretend that someone had told her.

5:30 p.m.
Jas is plucking my eyebrows. She said, "So what do you think I should do about Tom? Robbie says he still likes me, and that the girl at the dance was his cousin."

I said, "Oh, does that mean he can't get a girlfriend, then?"

Jas said (mid-pluck), "Georgie, don't start again. Do you think I should give him another chance?"

I thought, What am I, an agony aunt? But I said, "Well, maybe, but I'd play a bit hard to get. Don't kiss him on your first date... well, unless he really wants to."

Midnight
Got away surprisingly easily with the "It was Jas – I'm innocent!" plan re the dressing gown. Mum seems even

more mad than ever. And how long can it take to decorate one room? Jem is taking for ever. I'm not really surprised – he spends most of his time sitting around giggling with Mum. Libby called him "Dad" the other day.

Ho hum.

1:00 a.m.

Looking up at the sky from my bed I can hear an owl hooting and all is well with the world. Robbie is not engaged!!! Thank you, Baby Jesus.

Tuesday March 16th

3:00 p.m.

Miss Stamp says I show "promise" at tennis. It is very nice slamming the ball across the court past people. Or not past them, in Rosie's case, when it hit her in the face this afternoon. Her glasses went all sideways like Eric Morecambe which I thought was very funny. I couldn't serve for ages because of laughing so much.

10:45 p.m.

Woke up from a dream of winning Wimbledon. I think I

may be becoming sexually active, as the dream only really got interesting in the dressing room. First there was the usual stuff – you know, the final ace, the crowd going mad, going up for my trophy. Princess Margaret handing it over and saying, "Absolutely first class, most thrilling. It made me wish I still played."

Me saying, "Hahaha, I find it hard to believe you've ever played anything, Ma'am – except gin rummy." Then a quick wave and into the dressing room.

Once in the privacy of the changing room I began to get undressed for a well-deserved shower. When I had got down to my (well-filled D-cup) bra and knickers I was startled to find someone had come in the room. It was Leo DiCaprio. He said, "I'm sorry, did I startle you?" Then he started covering my quivering (but extremely fit and tanned) body with kisses. Just then someone else came in. I pulled away from Leo but Leo said, "It's OK, it's only Brad," and Brad Pitt came and joined us.

Monday March 22nd
2:00 p.m.

It's almost embarrassing how friendly Jas is being. A few days without my hilarious and witty conversation has reminded her of how much she likes me. In a roundabout way I suggested this to her on the way to school.

"Jas, I suppose a few days without my hilarious and witty conversation has reminded you of how much you like me."

She said, "Hahahaha..." but then saw my face and said, "Oh yes, how true. That will be it."

Wednesday March 31st
Assembly
9:08 a.m.

I nearly passed out with laughing this morning. As we were praying Rosie whispered, "Have a look at Jackie's nose, pass it on..." so the word passed right along the line. I couldn't see anything at first because Jackie had her head down and her hair was hanging over her face.

Then, as people were shuffling around to start the hymn, I went, "Jackie! Pssstt!" She looked up and round at me. The end of her nose was completely black!!! She looked like a panda in a wig. I almost wet myself it was so funny. Our whole line was shaking.

Jackie looked daggers at us but that only made it worse. There's nothing funnier than a really cross panda!! We staggered into the loos and were bent over the sinks, crying with laughter. At last, when I could speak, I said, "What... what... happened?"

Ellen said, "You know that DJ she was raving about? Well, he got drunk with his mates, came to meet Jackie and thought it would be very funny to give her a lovebite on the end of her nose."

Happy days.

The snogging report

Tuesday April 6th
5:00 p.m.
Had a game of tennis against Lucy Doyle from the fifth form and I beat her!!! I am a genius!!!

6:30 p.m.
Practising tennis against our wall at home but it's hopeless. Angus gets the ball and then takes it a few feet away from me and guards it. I go to get it and he waits until I can nearly get it and then he walks off with it again. I managed to hit him on the head with my tennis racquet but he doesn't seem to feel pain.

7:00 p.m.
Phoned Jas.

It's quite relaxing not having Dad around. No one bellowing, "Get off that bloody phone!" I'm beginning not to remember what he looks like.

So there's a silver lining to every cloud.

Jas's mum answered the phone and I asked to speak to Jas. She came down from her bedroom.

"Jas, I've got a good plan."

"Oh no."

"No, you'll like it."

"Why?"

"Because it's brilliant and also because it allows you to pay back your debt to me."

"Go on, then."

"Well, you know you said Robbie didn't know he was engaged, but Lindsay goes round with an engagement ring on...?"

"Yes."

"Well, if she only wears it at school and then takes it off when she sees him, well, that means that she likes him more than he likes her."

"I suppose."

"Of course it does. He must be getting tired of her by now – what on earth does he see in her?"

"She's supposed to be quite clever. I think she is applying for Oxford."

"So, she's a swot, that's no reason to like her – anyway, learning stuff is not clever. Just because I can't remember the Plantagenet line doesn't make me not clever."

"Well, no, I suppose."

"Exactly."

"You have quite a lot of trouble with quadratic equations as well."

"Yes, all right, Jas—"

"And you can't do the pluperfect tense—"

"Yes, I know, but what I'm saying is—"

"You're hopeless at German – Herr Kamyer said he's never known anyone so bad at it in all his years of teaching."

"Look, Jas, can we just get back to the plan? What I think we should do is to stalk Lindsay."

"Stalk her?"

"Yes."

"What... follow her around and then phone her up and ask her what colour panties she has got on?"

"No, not that bit, just the bit where we keep her under observation."

"Why? What is the point?"

"The point is, I will then be able to tell whether Robbie likes her or not."

"Why do I have to be involved?"

"Because a) you are my friend and b) it looks less suspicious because we are always hanging around together and c) my mum is going away with Libby in a few weeks and you could come and stay the night and we could invite Tom."

"When do we start stalking?"

That's my girl.

Friday April 16th
Operation stalking Lindsay begins
Friday night
4:15 p.m.

We had to hang around at the back of the science block after the final bell. Old Swotty Knickers (Lindsay) was chatting to Hawkeye. We could see them laughing together – how sad – fancy having to laugh with a teacher! Then, whilst Lindsay got her coat, we crept along the narrow alleyway that runs between the science block and the main school building. It is disgusting down there, full of fag-ends from Jackie and co. But if you follow it right along you end up a bit beyond the main gate. The tricky part is getting past Elvis's hut. I'd already made myself public enemy number one with him by putting a plastic skeleton with his hat on – and a pipe in its mouth – in his chair in his hut. I don't know how he knew it was me, but he did. Anyway, we got to Elvis's hut and he wasn't about so we shot across and into the last bit of the alleyway. We were wearing all black and had hats on – it was very like the French Resistance. We got to the end just as Lindsay (the stalkee) passed by. She looked at her watch and you could clearly see the flash of her ring.

5:15 p.m.
Outside Lindsay's posh house. The Yews.

The house is all on one level, which means that Lindsay's bedroom would be on the ground floor, which means we might be able to see in through the window.

Teeheee.

First things first, though, time for a nourishing meal.

6:30 p.m.

Double chips and Coke. Yum yum.

6:45 p.m.

Stalkee spotted leaving the front room, did not reappear. We suspect she has gone to her room to start the long, desperate job of making herself look OK to go out with Robbie.

6:58 p.m.

We decide to risk going round the back of the house. I whispered to Jas, "I hope they haven't got a cat."

And she said, "Don't you mean a dog?"

And I said, "Have you met Angus?"

There was a side path and we went really carefully down it. We had nearly reached the back garden when a head popped up from behind next door's hedge. A really bald head, like Uncle Eddie's. Quick as a flash, Jas said, "Sshhh, we are giving Lindsay a big surprise..." She winked at the man and he disappeared. We crept on round the back of the house. Lindsay's bedroom faced on to the garden and she had her curtains half pulled back so you could see in.

Her bedroom was a nightmare of frilly white things, frilly

pillows, frilly bedspread... Teletubby hot-water bottle cover!!!

Lindsay put on a tape and Jas and I looked at one another – it was Genesis. Jas mimed being sick. We had to keep bobbing our heads down if she turned directly to face the window. She disappeared off through another door and we could hear sort of gurgling noises. I said, "She's got an ensuite bathroom – that's very bad feng shui."

Jas said, "Why?"

And I said, "I don't know but it's very bad, you'd have to have about fifty goldfish to make it OK again... Have you seen her alarm clock? It's got a sleepy face on it."

Lindsay emerged from the bathroom with her hair all scraped back from her face and wearing a bra and a thong. I don't understand thongs – what is the point of them? I tried one of Mum's that she uses for aerobics... well, she is supposed to use it for aerobics but she only went once. She said that she nearly knocked herself out during the running on the spot because her breasts got out of hand. Anyway, I tried her thong on and it felt ridiculous... they just go up your bum as far as I can tell. Then I saw something even more grotesque. Lindsay didn't have any hair on her womanly parts! What had she done with it? She couldn't

185

have shaved it off, could she? I thought of the state of my legs the last time I had shaved them. I felt quite faint.

Lindsay was so skinny!! At least I filled my bra. Then, before our eyes, the stalkee did two things that were very significant and would have gone in our notebook had we had one:

1. She took off her ring and kissed it!!
2. She got some sort of pink rubber things and put them in her bra underneath her "breasts". The rubber things pushed up her "breasts" and made it look like she had a cleavage. What a swiz.

I said to Jas, "I bet you Robbie doesn't know about that..."

But I noticed that I did not have Jas's full attention, she was looking over my shoulder at Mr Baldy-man, who had reappeared, peering at us over his fence. What is it with neighbours, don't they have lives of their own? He seemed a bit suspicious. So I said as naturally as I could. "She's certainly playing her music very loudly – she hasn't heard us tapping on her window. Do it again, Jas." Jas looked a bit stunned but fortunately had the presence of mind to do some mime. She mimed tapping on the window, then she mimed waving at Lindsay (who fortunately had gone back into the ensuite) and then she mimed hysterical laughter.

It's very tiring, this stalking business, but we seemed to satisfy Mr Baldy-man because he disappeared again and we crept round to the front of the house and along to the big hedge next door. We hid just inside next door's driveway to wait for Lindsay to come out.

7:40 p.m.

Brrrr... bit chilly. At last the front door opened and Lindsay came out with her hair up (mistake) and in a black midi (mistake for long-streak-of-water type person). We huddled back into the shadows of the hedge as she passed and gave her a few minutes before we followed. When she got to the main street she stood under a streetlamp and got out a compact to look at herself. Instead of running screaming home, she snapped the compact shut and walked on.

Suddenly I had the feeling that we were doing something wrong. Up until now I had been caught up in my French Resistance fantasy but what if I found out something I didn't want to know? What if she met Robbie and it was quite obvious that he really liked her? Could I stand it? Did I want to see him kissing her? I said to Jas, "Maybe we should go now."

And Jas said, "What, after all this? No way. I want to see what happens next."

7:50 p.m.
Outside the Odeon Robbie was waiting. My heart went all wobbly, he looked so cool. Why wasn't he mine? Lindsay went up to him. The moment of truth. I wanted to yell out, "She has bits of pink rubber down her bra... and she wears a thong!!!"

I held my breath and Jas's hand. She whispered, "Get off, you lezzer." Then... Lindsay put her face forward and Robbie kissed her.

8:00 p.m.
Walking home, eating more chips, I said, "What sort of kiss do you think it was? Was there actual lip contact? Or was it lip to cheek, or lip to corner of mouth?"

"I think it was lip to corner of mouth, but maybe it was lip to cheek?"

"It wasn't full-frontal snogging though, was it?"

"No."

"I think she went for full-frontal and he converted it into lip to corner of mouth."

"Yes."

"He didn't seem keen though, did he?"

"No."

"Didn't you think so either?"

"No."

"No, neither did I."

Outside Jas's gate
8:40 p.m.

I said, "The facts are a) she doesn't wear her ring when she is out with him, so that makes it clear that she says they are engaged but they are not, and b) he doesn't really rate her because he didn't do full-frontal with her."

Jas undid her gate. "Yes. Right, see you tomorrow. Don't forget to fix the sleepover."

Midnight

So... the plot thickens. All I have to do is get rid of Lindsay, convince Robbie I am the woman of his dreams, stop Mum splitting up the home, grow bigger breasts and have plastic surgery on my nose and I have cracked it...

Thursday April 29th

6:30 p.m.

Phone rang and I answered it. A strange voice said, "G'day, is that Georgie?" I was a bit formal – it might be a dirty phone call. (I had had one of those from a phone box in Glasgow. This bloke with a Scottish accent kept saying, "What colour pa—?" and then the pips would go and I'd say, "I'm sorry, what did you say?" and then he'd start again. "What colour panties...?" pip pip pip. Eventually he managed to say, "What colour panties have you got on?" and then the line went dead. So you can't be too careful.)

This strange, echoey voice said, "It's your dad, I'm calling from Whangamata."

I was a bit surprised and I said, "Oh-er-hello-Dad."

He was all enthusiastic and keen. "How's school?"

"Oh, you know... school."

"Is everyone all right?"

"Yes. Angus got next door's guinea pig."

"Did he give it back?"

"He did when I hit him with my tennis racquet."

"And Libby?"

"She can say 'tosser' now."

"Who the hell taught her that?"

"I don't know."

"Well, you should take better care of her."

"She's not my bloody daughter."

"Don't swear at me."

"I only said bloody."

"That's swear— look, look, get your mum on the phone, this is costing me one pound a minute."

"She's not here."

"Where is she?"

"Oh, I don't know, she's always out."

"Well, tell her I called."

"OK."

There was a bit of silence then. His voice sounded even weirder when he spoke again. "I wish you were all here, I miss you."

I just went, "Hmmmpgh."

I wish parents wouldn't do that, you know, make you feel like crying and hitting them at the same time.

I use it to keep my balls still

Tuesday May 4th

8:10 a.m.

Felt a bit sort of down in the dumps when I woke up. I'd had a dream that my dad had grown a Rolf Harris beard but it wasn't a beard really, it was Angus clinging to his chin.

Assembly. Maths. Physics... there is not one part of today that is worth being alive for.

4:30 p.m.

Home, exhausted from laughing. My ribs hurt. Slim has made me be on cloakroom duty for the next term but I don't care, it was worth it.

Well... here is what happened. It was during double physics and it was just one of those afternoons when you can't stop laughing and you feel a bit hysterical. For most of the lesson I had been yelling, "*Jawohl*, Herr Kommandant!"

and clicking my heels together every time Herr Kamyer asked if we understood what he had been explaining. We were doing the molecular structure of atoms and how they vibrate.

Herr Kamyer was illustrating his point with the aid of some billiard balls on a tea towel on his desk. It was giving me the giggles anyway, and then I put my hand up because I had thought of a good joke. I put my hand up with the finger pointing forward, like in "Who ate all the pies?" and when Herr Kamyer said, "Yes?" I said, "Herr Kamyer, what part does the tea towel play in the molecular structure?"

That is when Herr Kamyer made his fateful mistake – he said, "Ach, no, I merely use the tea towel to keep my balls still." It was pandemonium. I could not stop laughing. You know when you really, really should stop laughing because you will get into dreadful trouble if you don't? But you still can't stop? Well, I had that. I had to be practically carried to Slim's office. Outside her office I did my best to get a grip and I thought I had just about stopped and was under control when I knocked on the door and she said, "Come."

In my head I was thinking, Please, please don't ask me anything about it. Just let it go. Please talk about something else, just don't ask me about it. Please please.

Slim was all trembly and jelloid. "Can you tell me, Georgia, what is quite so amusing about Herr Kamyer's experiment on the vibration of atoms?"

I tried. God knows, I tried. "Well, Miss Simpson, it's just that he used a tea towel... he used a tea towel..."

"Yes?"

"He used a tea towel to... keep his balls still." And then I was off again.

Midnight
Bloody funny, though.

Thursday May 27th
Tennis tournament
2:30 p.m.
Through to the semifinals. Beautiful sunny day. I think I will be a Wimbledon champion after all. White suits me. All the gang are cheering me on and this is very freaky deaky and karmic and weird but... if I win my semi against Kirsty Walsh (upper fifth) I will play Lindsay in the final. How weird is that? Pretty weird, that's what. Lindsay is such a

boring player, I'm sure I could beat her. She plays by the book... baseline follow through to the net, but she hasn't met Mighty Lob (me) yet.

OK, if I beat her that must mean I am meant to have Robbie. Lindsay has white frilly knickers on under her tennis skirt. (Not the thong, thank goodness, otherwise Miss Stamp might have had an outburst of lesbian lust and put me off my game.) I think my shorts are much more stylish. They look like I've just remembered I'm playing in a tennis final and I've just grabbed something and thrown it on in an attractive way.

3:30 p.m.

I won the first set and now I'm serving for the second and the match.

I feel pretty good. I'm a bit hot but I feel confident about my serve. Rosie and Ellen and Jools and Jas and all of my year are going mental. Chanting my name and "Easy, easy." Hawkeye keeps telling them to be quiet. (She is the umpire, worse luck.)

But even she can't make me lose. Hahahaha. I am ruler of the universe. Robbie is mine for the plucking.

195

First serve – an ACE!!! Yes! Yes! Yesssss!! Hawkeye says, "Fifteen-love."

Second serve – a brief rally and then a cunning, slicing cross-court forehand from me. Hawkeye says, "Thirty-love."

Third service. Whizzzz. Oh yes, another ace!! Kirsty was nowhere. What a Slack Alice. C'mon if you think you're hard enough!!!!

Hawkeye says, "Forty-love."

The whole court is hushed as I serve for the match. I take my place behind the baseline. Jas is playing nervously with her fringe. I looked at her. She stops.

I throw the ball up and bring my racquet down, putting a bit of top spin on it. Kirsty doesn't even try to get it. ACE!!!!

Hawkeye announces through tight lips, "Game, set and match to Georgia Nicolson." Yesss!!!!! Victory!!!!!!

I fall to my knees like McEnroe and the crowd is going mad. Full of euphoria I fling my racquet high up into the air.

It curves and falls down and hits Hawkeye right on the head. She is knocked off her umpire chair, unconscious.

In bed

8:00 p.m.

I CAN'T BELIEVE IT. Hawkeye was only unconscious for about a minute but I was made to forfeit the match. Kirsty played Lindsay. I couldn't bear to watch – more to the point, I wasn't allowed to watch – I had to go and tidy all the gym mats.

Lindsay won the cup.

I don't know what this means karmically. I don't think I believe in God any more.

11:00 p.m.

The only way I will believe in God is if something really bloody great happens to me soon.

Pyjama party

Friday June 4th
The pyjama party sleepover
5:00 p.m.

Mum will not get going. Why is she so slow? Libby still has not got any knickers on. I offer to put them on her and Mum says, "Oh, would you, love? Thanks. I cannot find my eyebrow tweezers anywhere. You haven't seen them, have you?"

(I remember they are in my pencil case.) "Er... no, but I think I saw Libby with them."

"Damn, they could be anywhere."

Libby decided that "knickers on" was a game and I chased her around for ages before I could get hold of her. Then when I was putting her knick-knacks on she was stroking my hair, going, "Prrr prr. Nice pussycat. Do you want some milk, tosser?" I think she thinks "tosser" is like a name.

Once I got her dressed I raced upstairs and got the tweezers, then I put them in Angus's basket. (Fortunately he was out murdering birds or he would have eaten them.) Then I shouted to Mum, "Hey, Mum, guess where your tweezers are? Come and see!"

Mum came out of the bedroom and I pointed to the cat basket. She said, "Honestly!! Thanks, love. Right now, I think that's everything. We can get off now, Libby."

She grabbed Libby, who was struggling and licking her face. Libby said, "Bad, bad Mummy, stealing Libby."

As they went through the door Mum said, "You'll be OK, won't you? I'll be back late tomorrow – eat something sensible and don't stay up too late."

She went through the door and then came back a moment later. "Don't even think about doing anything to your hair."

6:00 p.m.

Rosie was the first to arrive. She said, "Sven is going to come at about eleven thirty, after his restaurant shift finishes."

I said, "What have you got up to with him?"

She said, "Er... six and a bit of seven..."

We had this scoring system for kissing and so on, from one to ten:

1. holding hands
2. arm around
3. goodnight kiss
4. kiss lasting over three minutes without a breath
5. open mouth kissing
6. tongues
7. upper body fondling – outdoors
8. upper body fondling – indoors (in bed)
9. below waist activity
10. the full monty

I said, "What is he like at it?"

Rosie said, "He's good, I think Danish boys are better at it than English ones. They change rhythm more."

I said, "What do you mean?"

"You know English boys get really excited and just sort of kiss with the same pressure? Well, he varies the pressure: sometimes it's gentle and sometimes hard and then middley."

I said, "Oh, I like that."

Rosie said, "I know, I do too. Apparently all girls do. We like variety whereas boys like the same."

I said, "How do you know that?" and she looked a bit smug. "It's in *Men are from Mars, Women are from Venus*."

Jools, Ellen, Jas, Patty, Sarah and Mabs all turned up and we got out our jimjams. We watched *Grease* and kept stopping it and doing bits from it. I did "You're The One That I Want" on the sofa.

Then, at about eleven o'clock, the phone rang. I answered and it was Tom wanting to speak to Jas. So Jas went off into the hall and shut the door so we couldn't hear. When she came back her face was a bit pink. She sort of croaked, "He's coming round with his mate Leo... ohmyGodohmyGod ohmyGod!"

11:30 p.m.

Eating toast and Pop-Tarts when Leo and Tom arrived. They brought their pyjamas too and put them on. What a good laugh. Then Sven turned up – I'd forgotten how big he is... Rosie and he disappeared off and the rest of us watched

Grease again. This time the boys joined in. Tom is quite a laugh. I desperately tried not to mention Robbie.

1:00 a.m.
Still up and chatting about EVERYTHING!!!! Haven't seen Rosie and Sven for hours. Surely they must have got past seven by now???

1:30 a.m.
Tom and Jas disappeared off and Leo and Ellen went off "to get some air". Why they think there is no air in the lounge, I don't know. The rest of us Normans (Norman no mates) decided to dare each other. It started off with taking your knickers off and putting them on your head, and so on, and then I dared Sarah to go and stand on the garden wall and drop her pyjama trousers and knickers.

She did.

2:00 a.m.
Patty and Mabs dared me to streak down to the bottom of the street. They said they would buy me a new lipstick if I did. The "couples" were still away so I thought I'd do it. We

went outside (us Normans), all in our jimjams. It was a nice summer night, and there were no houselights on in the streets except for ours. So I took my jimjams off and ran like mad in my nuddy-pants down to the bottom of the street and back. It made us die laughing – the others couldn't believe that I had done it!!!

We were all collapsed on the front doorstep when the "couples" came back. I hid behind the others whilst I scrambled into my pyjamas. Tom winked at me. "I should tell my brother what he's missing."

I went purple. "Don't you dare, Tom. Promise, promise me you won't!!"

Tom said, "Do you think that me and Jas should go out with each other again?"

I said, "Oh yes!! I think you are perfect for each other."

And he said, "I've always liked you because you are so sincere."

At about two thirty the lads went home and we cleared up the house. Please don't let Tom tell Robbie about the nuddy-pants incident.

All us girls snuggled up under duvets in the front room, chatting about everything – boys, make-up... lesbians.

Rosie said, "How do you get to become a lesbian?"

I said, "Why? Are you going to give it a go?"

Jas said, "You can't just give it a go. You can't just think, Oh, I'll give being a lesbian a go."

Ellen sat up. "A go at what?"

Jas went a bit red (which is a lot red in anyone else's language). "Well, have a go at, er, snogging a girl."

We all sat up then and went "Erlacck!"

Rosie said, "Is that what they do, then – snog each other?"

Jas (the lesbian spokesperson) said a bit smugly, "Of course they do. They have proper sexual wotsits."

Rosie said, "How can they have proper sexual wotsits when they haven't got... you know, any proper sexual wotsits."

I interrupted, "Jas, how come you know so much about it, anyway?"

She went ludicrously red. Rosie had got all interested now. "But, I mean, what do they do when they haven't got proper sexual wotsits?"

I said to Jas, "Go on, then, Miss Expert Knickers. What do they do in the privacy of their own lesbian love-nests?"

And Jas sort of mumbled something under her duvet. I

said, "You don't know, do you?" and she mumbled again, "Snnubbing."

I repeated, "Snubbing. They do snubbing? They snub each other?"

Jas sat up and said, "No, rubbing."

I said "Goodnight" really quickly and we all went to sleep.

Wednesday June 16th
6:00 p.m.

Got a note from Jackie today: *We are knocking off school this afternoon and going down town to "get a few things". We'll tell you all about the plan at lunch.*

I knew that "getting a few things" meant shoplifting in Jackiespeak. I tried to hide from her at lunchtime but she found me in the loos. I was reading my mag in one of the cubicles – I had my feet off the ground so you couldn't see there was anyone there but she went into the next-door cubicle and looked over the top of the loo wall.

She said, "What are you doing?"

I didn't look up, I just said, "I'm practising origami."

She said, "Are you ready to go? We've got lists of what to

get and where we will meet later."

Suddenly I snapped. I really was sick to death of her and Alison, they didn't make me laugh or anything, they just kept making me do things I didn't want to do. I was sick of it. I found myself saying, "I'm not coming and I don't think you should go either."

Jackie was amazed. "Have you become a Christian? I haven't seen your tambourine. Come on, get your coat and we'll go over the back fields."

I said, "No," and came out of the cubicle. She followed me and came up close – she is quite big.

She said, "I think you had better." Alison was just behind her.

Then this odd calm voice came out of me. I'd been watching *Xena, Warrior Princess* and for one stupid moment I thought I was her. I said, "Oh good, I didn't realise I'd be able to try out my new martial arts skills so soon. If I break anything I apologise in advance. I've only practised on bricks before."

Jackie looked a bit puzzled (who wouldn't?) but she kept coming nearer and suddenly with a yell I grabbed her arm and twisted it right up her back. I don't know how.

But I was doing it for the little people everywhere (I don't mean dwarfs – I just mean, you know, vulnerable people).

8:00 p.m.
Jas phoned. "Everyone is talking about you – it's brilliant!!"

8:30 p.m.
I am cock of the walk. (I don't know what the girl equivalent of "cock" is... surely it can't be "vagina". I am vagina of the walk doesn't have the same ring to it, somehow...)

Midnight
Yesssss!!!!!

Saturday June 19th
9:00 a.m.
The Stiff Dylans are playing at The Market Place. Tom and Jas are going, and all the gang. Shall I?

11:30 a.m.
Mum is being ridiculous – she refuses to let me dye my hair

blonde. I said, "Where would Marilyn Monroe have been if Mrs Monroe had said, 'No, Marilyn, you'll ruin your hair'?"

Mum said, "Don't be ridiculous."

But I went on, "And what about Caprice?... Do you suppose Mrs Caprice said—"

Mum threw her slipper at me. Oh great, now she has turned to violence. I may yet ring Esther Rantzen's childline.

2:00 p.m.
Nngut naface-musk on, I cnt muv mi face.

2:30 p.m.
Blocked the sink with my egg-yolk mask.

4:00 p.m.
I'm going to start my make-up now.

4:30 p.m.
Double *merde*. I'll have to start all over again, I've stuck the mascara brush in my eye. It's all watery and red.

5:30 p.m.

Lying down with cucumber slices on my eyes to take down the swelling.

5:50 p.m.

Libby crept in and ate one of my cucumber slices. It gave me a terrible shock to see her face looming over me when I wasn't expecting it.

6:00 p.m.

Ellen rang, we are meeting outside The Market Place at eight thirty.

Midnight

What an unbelievably BRILLIANT night. Double cool with knobs. Robbie KISSED me. The Sex God has landed. It was so mega.

The Stiff Dylans played some great music and Jas, Tom, Leo, Ellen and me worked out these funny dance routines. Lindsay was there, all po-faced. Robbie was great in the band. I felt a bit self-conscious about dancing at first but then I began to enjoy myself. I showed Tom and Jas a little routine I had made up in my bedroom – and then it was like in a film because everyone – loads of people – started copying it and joining in.

I was a bit out of breath at the end and hot, so when the band took a break I went outside the back door. There was this sort of patio area. As I was standing there Robbie came out... I felt really awkward and was going to go back in when he put his arm on mine and said, "Can I just speak to you for a minute, Georgia?"

I said, "Yes, fine..." He looked a bit embarrassed so I said, "Look, if it's about Jas and Tom I'm sorry that you were angry with me... I think he's really nice and Jas likes him a lot."

Robbie said, "Well, I'm glad, but it's not that. I've just been meaning to give you this." Then he kissed me!!!! I went completely jelloid – it was like being part girl, part jellyfish. It was mega brilliant. Twenty out of ten type kissing. I got all that stuff you're supposed to have – fireworks whooshing in your head, bands playing, sea crashing in and out... I don't know how long it went on for, I was so faint.

Eventually he said, "I've wanted to do that for a long time, but I know it's wrong."

I could hardly speak, it came out all mad. "Ng ng –'s OK, not wrong, no wrong, ngng ng – I mean it's, I, what I, you and, always, even when I ng." He looked at me as if I was talking a foreign language. But I wasn't, I was just talking rubbish.

Then one of the lads in the band came out and Robbie sort of leaped away from me like a leaping thing. Then he went back in, saying to me, "OK, so Georgia, will you pass that on to Tom? See you later."

"See you later?" What does that mean? Here we go again!!!

I told Jas and she said, "What's going to happen now? Are you his bit on the side? What does he mean, 'See you later'? Does he mean see you later or see you later?" I had to stick my hand over her mouth to shut her up. When Robbie took the stage again I had to stop myself gazing at him like an idiot. He was so gorgeous and he had kissed me!!

When the gig was over Robbie passed by me and said, "I'll call you." Then he went over to Lindsay. She put her arms round his neck and I couldn't watch any more.

When will he call me?

Angus was in my bed when I got home, and Libby. I had

to sleep in a sort of S-shape with my feet hanging out of the bed. But I don't care!!!!

Tuesday June 22nd

5:10 p.m.

I don't know if it's me or the weather but I am so hot all the time.

No call for three days.

Wednesday June 23rd

11:00 p.m.

No call today.

Thursday June 24th

6:00 p.m.

Phoned Jas.

"He's not called yet."

Jas said, "Look, leave it with me. I'll try to find out something from Tom."

"Will you do it subtly though, Jas?"

She said, "What do you take me for? I know what's subtle."

And I said, "Well, I'm sorry, but I feel a bit sensitive and I don't want anyone to know about it until I know what is going on myself."

She said, "Look, relax, my middle name is 'cool'."

I said, "Is it? I thought it was Pollyanna."

She said, "Well, it is, my mum liked the film, but that's not what I mean – and anyway, you said you'd never mention that I told you that."

I said, "OK, but just remember to be subtle, all right?"

She said, "Of course. Hang on a minute." Then I heard her yelling up the stairs, "Mum, will you ask Tom to come down here!"

I heard a bit of faraway noise then Jas's mum yelling from upstairs, "Tom says what do you want? He has just set up the computer and can't come away at the moment."

Then I heard Jas yell back, "Well, will you say that Robbie kissed Georgia and said he would call her later and he hasn't called her yet. Does he know anything about it?"

I couldn't believe my ears and it got worse because Jas's mum joined in, "Robbie kissed Georgie – but he's going out with Lindsay, isn't he?"

Jas yelled back, "Yes, but he's confused."

Then I heard Tom yelling down, "What kind of kiss was it?"

And Jas said, "I think it was six."

I REALLY WANTED TO KILL HER.

"Jas, Jas, SHUT UP!!!"

Friday June 25th

1:00 p.m.

Lindsay came up to me at lunch break. She's so wet close up, she's got really blinky blue watery eyes like a blue-eyed bat. Anyway, old blinky said, "I've heard what happened on Saturday."

I went a bit pale. "You've heard what?" I played for time.

"I heard that you have been going after my boyfriend."

How dare she suggest that I would do such a thing!! I went red and said, "What idiot has been saying that?"

Lindsay glared at me. "Robbie told me." I couldn't take it in. She went on, "He told me how you followed him at the break and then you just flung yourself on him. He said he was sorry for you but also very embarrassed."

I spluttered, I couldn't speak. She went on, "So I'm giving you a warning – don't be so sad. You're a silly little girl, don't let it happen again." I couldn't help thinking of the Ancient

Egyptians – they used to put long-handled spoons up people's noses and scoop their brains out. Of course, the people were dead first but in Lindsay's case there was hardly any difference between alive and dead. I was going to get some spoons and poke them up her beastly, sticky-up nose.

6:00 p.m.

Jas is going to gang up on Lindsay with me. I said to her, "Do you think Robbie really said I was sad and I flung myself on him?"

Jas was a real pal. "No, no, of course not... er... you didn't, did you?"

6:30 p.m.

Oh why this? Why would he be such a pig as to say that? Oh I hate him, I hate him.

Midnight

I hate him, I hate him.

12:30 a.m.

Oh I love him, I love him.

The sex god has landed

Thursday July 1st
Canteen
1:00 p.m.

Lindsay put her coffee cup down while she went to get her bag and I spat in it (the coffee cup, not her bag – although I will spit in her bag if I get the chance). I hate her.

Jackie and Alison get on my nerves even more now they have decided to be my friends. Jackie bought me a bar of chocolate today. It will be an apple next. It's a pathetic world when twisting someone's arm up their back gets them buying you things.

4:00 p.m.

I'm so angry with Robbie. I want to tell him what I think about him but I have too much pride.

4:30 p.m.

Phoned Robbie at home (I got the number from Jas). He answered the phone but I just slammed down the receiver. (And I had done one-four-one as well, haha hahaha.)

4:45 p.m.

Phoned Robbie.

He answered and I said, "Robbie, it's Georgia."

He sort of breathed out and then he said, "Er... I can't really find that science paper you asked me about, Mike, can I call you later? Thanks. Bye."

4:50 p.m.

Phoned Jas. "What does he mean by calling me Mike?"

Jas said, "Well, I suppose Lindsay must have been there."

5:30 p.m.

In bed with the curtains closed.

5:45 p.m.

Mum came into my room.

She said, "Do you want to talk about anything?"

I said, "Yes, suicide."

She said, "It can't be as bad as that."

I said, "Well it is, it's worse. I don't want to be here any more. I hate school. I hate England."

She said, "Well, do you think that maybe a summer trip to New Zealand might cheer you up? We could go over to Disneyland on the way."

I said, "I don't care what I do."

6:30 p.m.

So this is what men are like. Well, that is it, then. I am going to be a lesbian.

7:00 p.m.

I got out some photos of Denise Van Outen and tried to imagine kissing her.

7:05 p.m.

I can't do it. And I can't help thinking about Miss Stamp's moustache. And the rubbing.

7:10 p.m.

I'll have to be a nun, then.

8:00 p.m.

It's no use, if I pull all my hair back like a nun, it makes my nose look huge. Still, I don't suppose that matters when you are only saving poor people and making soup for them, like nuns do.

9:00 p.m.

The phone rang for me. I said to Mum, "Who is it?" and she said, "I don't know, it's a boy."

9:30 p.m.

Robbie is going to meet me tomorrow after school at my house. He was in a phone box and said that he couldn't really explain, he'd talk tomorrow. If he thinks he can "explain" this away he's very much mistaken. I have got some pride. I've got a lot to say to him about his "explanation"!!!

9:45 p.m.

What shall I wear? Maybe I won't go to school tomorrow to give myself time to get made up in a natural way.

Friday July 2nd
8:05 a.m.

Said goodbye to Mum and Libbs and went as normal to Jas's. She was waiting for me on the corner. I said, "I'm not coming to school today, I'm meeting Robbie. Will you say that I have got the painters in very badly? Thanks."

Then I went back home. I waited until Mum and Libbs left and then I slipped back into the house.

Day plan:

1. Steam face.
2. Apply face pack.
3. Sort out clothes to wear.
4. Tidy bedroom (well, put everything on the floor and then under the bed).
5. Put some interesting books near my bed (hide comics and boy mags).
6. Remove nuddy-pants poster of Reeves and Mortimer.

7. Make sure Libby has not peed or pooed in any secret corner.

11:00 a.m.

In my room tidying when I heard the front door open. If it was a burglar I only had Mum's tweezers to defend myself with. Where was Angus when you needed him? I hadn't seen the mad furry thing for hours.

11:02 a.m.

Not burglars, it's something much worse... it's Mum. And she's not alone! She has Jem the decorator with her. Oh fabulous, my mum is having an affair with a builder. Also she is older than him – also I already have a dad, who is bad enough, but better the dad you know than the builder you don't.

They went into the lounge so I crept downstairs to see if I could hear what was going on. I put my ear against the door but I couldn't quite hear. I pressed my ear quite hard up against the keyhole. I heard Jem say, "This is the door that sticks. I'm going to—" and that's when he opened the door and I crashed into the room.

221

Noon

In bed. I had to pretend that I had fainted. I lay still on the floor until Mum put something disgusting (smelling salts) under my nose. I thought my head was going to come off. I sort of pretended that I was all confused and that I had felt ill on the way to school.

Mum made me come to bed with an aspirin. Soon after, I heard the door slam. Mum came up. "Er – I just took an hour off to discuss the final details about the lounge with Jem."

I said, "He's taken about a hundred years to decorate one room. Libby thinks he is our new dad."

Mum laughed. "Don't be so silly, why would you think she thought that?"

I said, "Because she calls him 'my new dad'."

Mum ignored that and went on, "Well, I must get back to work, are you sure you will be all right?"

I said, "Oh yes, I'll be all right – will YOU be all right?" (I said it really meaningfully but she didn't know what I meant.)

Minutes later she came back in the room and said, "Georgia, I know that you like a bit of drama, but I'm afraid that Jem and I are not having a passionate affair."

I said, "Oh, what is it then? A really lukewarm affair?"

She sat down on my bed. "It's not any kind of affair. Look, love, I really, really miss your dad." And it was horrible because her eyes were all leaky.

I said, "You can't miss his moustache."

She said, "No, I don't miss that. But I love him. Don't you?"

I said, "He's all right."

She kissed me. "I know you do love him, you're just moody and someone has to suffer, but never mind, we'll be seeing him soon."

Then she left. God, I can't stand this having to talk about grown-ups all the time! I do wish my dad was here, then I could forget all about him!

4:00 p.m.

Robbie will be here in half an hour. I'd better just go to the loo again. I've only been ten times in the last ten minutes. I hope I'm not incontinent, I'll have to wear big nappies... Robbie will never stand for that – if he gets famous he won't want a girlfriend who wears nappies.

♡ 223

Robbie has just gone. I feel all hollow inside like a hollowed-out coconut. He looked gorgeous, all in black, and sort of sad. He gave me a brilliant smile when he saw me and then he just pulled me towards him (quite roughly, actually...). I remembered how cross I was though, so I only snogged him for half an hour before I said, "How could you tell Lindsay that I was sad and that I followed you outside and flung myself on you?"

He looked puzzled. "I didn't say that."

"Didn't you?"

"No, I didn't... I haven't said anything to anyone."

"Well, that's what Lindsay said to me."

He looked uncomfortable.

I went on, "And are you engaged to her or not?"

He looked really puzzled then. "Engaged to her? Why should you think that?"

"Well, because she wears an engagement ring at school that she tells people you gave her."

He sat down. "This is bad."

I tried to go on being cross but he looked so gorgey porgey that I couldn't keep it up. Then he looked right into my eyes. I tried not to blink because not blinking is supposed to be attractive. He said, "Look Georgie, I'm having real trouble with this. The truth is, I've been trying to find a way to end it with Lindsay but I don't want to hurt her feelings."

I said, "Yes, it's tricky, isn't it? Because she obviously likes you a lot. Still, I've got an idea..."

He looked hopeful. "What is it?"

"I'll tell her, in a nice way of course, that she is a wet weed and that she is dumped. That should do it."

He did actually laugh! He said, "You're mad. Anyway, it's my problem and I'll sort it out, but there is something else I have to tell you."

Here it comes, I was thinking (but not blinking). He's going to say, "You are the girl of my dreams, will you be my girlfriend? You are the most gorgeous girl I have ever—"

I'd just got to that bit in my head when he interrupted me. "I have to tell you, it wouldn't be fair to you not to... but well, I am attracted to you (I tried not to smirk or smile too much in case he had second thoughts when he saw my nose spreading all over my face) but I can't go out with you."

I said, "Why not?"

And he said, "Because you are too young. I'm nearly

eighteen – it would not be right, it would be like cradle-snatching."

I argued with him. I even said, "I'm not really fourteen, I'm actually fifteen and a half, it's just that I'm not very bright and they've kept me back a year."

He laughed, but in a sad way. Then he gave me a last kiss sort of thing and went.

Midnight
Too young for him. Oh *merde merde merde, double merde.*

I wonder where Angus is? I could do with something to cuddle even if I did get a savage biting.

Monday July 5th
11:30 a.m.
Mucho excitemondo!!! Robbie has dumped Lindsay!!! Hurrah!!! She came into school with her eyes all swollen up like little boiled sweets. I passed her in the corridor and she said, "I hope you're satisfied now, you horrid little girl." Horrid little girl, that's nice.

I could have said, "At least I don't wear bits of rubber down my bra and a piece of string up my bottom." But unfortunately I began to feel a bit sorry for her – after all, she would never get another boyfriend, whereas even if I had to wait a whole year I would one day be older and then I could get Robbie.

5:30 p.m.
I'm glum, though – a year seems a long, long time and what if he finds someone else before I get old enough?

6:30 p.m.
Still no sign of Angus. This is a bit unusual. He always comes back for his dindins.

7:00 p.m.
Looking round the street for Angus. I had a dead mouse and a chop to entice him.

7:15 p.m.
Just stumbled into Mark, snogging in his driveway with some girl... he's always at it!! If it's true that stimulation makes things bigger (breasts etc.), perhaps he had very tiny lips when he was born and he has just overstimulated

them by snogging all the time.

9:30 p.m.
No Angus. I hoped he might be at home lurking behind the curtain ready to attack my legs, but he's not.

11:00 p.m.
No phone calls, no Angus. Libby came into bed with me. "Where big pussy tosser?" she asked me. I almost cried. I really cuddled her but it made her too cross and she bit me on the chin.

Had a dream about Robbie. I had blonde hair in the dream.

Tuesday July 6th
7:30 p.m.
Eureka!!! I've got it!!! I know what my dream was trying to tell me. There is a way I can convince Robbie that I am more mature than my fourteen years... I have to dye a blonde streak in my hair. A blonde streak will add years to my appearance!!!

Still no sign of Angus. Mum said, "I don't want to upset

you, but you know that he stalks cars and attacks them – it may be that this time he's had a bit of an accident."

I can't bear to think of this.

Midnight

I think of all the animals in the world and all the sad things that happen to them. Little chickens whose parents go for a day's outing on the farmyard truck and never come back because they have gone to be on somebody's table. And all the little sheep who see their mummies and daddies loaded into vans... oh I cannot stand this. I'm never going to eat meat again.

1:00 a.m.

They say vegetables feel pain. What about the little baby potatoes all snug underground with their brother and sister potatoes and then a big hand comes and uproots them and... slices them up. Oh God, now I can never eat chips again.

2:30 a.m.

What can I eat, then?

♡ 229

4:00 a.m.
If I starved myself to death I wonder if Robbie would think I was grown-up enough?

Wednesday July 7th

8:00 a.m.
I'm shattered this morning, and upset. I miss Angus. Even Mum does. Mrs Next Door doesn't, though. When I asked her if she had seen him, she said, "No I haven't. And I know he hasn't been in my yard because nothing is dead or dug up and my dog is not a nervous wreck." I hate her – I hope her husband gets stuck in his greenhouse and then she will know what I feel like. She will know what true pain is.

And suffering.

2:30 p.m.
Ink fight in RE, which generally cheers me up, but I couldn't even flick properly I was so upset.

The gossip at school is that Lindsay is not eating and has got what's it – anorexia. I don't know how you would know, she's so skinny anyway.

Nearly the summer hols, so it will be the last I see of this hell-hole for a bit.

Friday July 9th
8:50 p.m.
I really think Angus must have been run over or something. I miss him, we've been through a lot of stuff, me and him. Stupid furry freak. But I love him. It seems I am destined to lose everything I love.

Sunday July 11th
2:00 p.m.
Jas and I looked in all the streets around her house, just in case Angus had followed me one day and then lost his way. We were just by her place when Robbie pulled up in his mini. He looked a bit ruffled but I was too down in the dumps to think about it much. He said, "Have you found Angus?"

I said, "No, we've looked everywhere."

Wednesday July 14th
3:30 p.m.
Every cloud has a bit of a silver lining. I was sitting against

the school wall in the shade, just thinking. The others were all sprawled out in their knickers sunbathing by the tennis courts. The bit of wall I was leaning against was just near Elvis's hut. I saw him put on his coat and get his shopping bag... what a wally he looked. He closed the hut door but he didn't lock it and then he went off. I'd nothing else to do so I thought I'd go and sit in his hut for a while, see what it would be like to be a school caretaker.

There was nothing much in the hut – a chair and a table and a little fridge and some magazines he's been reading. I sat down and flicked through them... and my jaw nearly dropped off. Because they were naughty magazines, if you know what I mean. Called *Fiesta* and *Big Girls*. One of them was called *Down Your Way*, and was all full of candid photos of readers and their wives in the privacy of their own bedrooms. Some of them were so fat!! I flicked through the pages to the centrefold. And the centrefold was ELVIS and MRS ELVIS!!!! In the NUDDY-PANTS!!!! I couldn't believe it. Elvis in the nuddy-pants. Elvis was standing by the kettle in the nuddy-pants, pretending to make a cup of tea and Mrs Elvis was doing the washing-up in the nuddy-pants!!!

I took the mag with me and passed it around the whole

class. We were laughing for the whole afternoon, someone only had to say, "Fancy a cup of tea, my dear?" and we'd be off again. Ooohhhhh, it made my stomach really hurt with laughing.

Elvis knows someone has got his mag but he can't say anything. If I see him I just let my eyes drift down to his trousers...

Saturday July 17th
12:00 p.m.

Joy joy, double bubble joy. Hadihahahaha. Robbie has just phoned me. He has found Angus!! Robbie had been out searching for him and he heard all these dogs barking so he went to see what they were barking at. And it was Angus, tied up. Some people had found him, he had a bad paw so they had bandaged it up and tied him up until they found his owners. They had put up notices but I hadn't seen them.

Robbie said the people were bloody glad to get rid of him as he had already eaten two doormats and a clothesline. They were lucky they got off so lightly.

Anyway, Robbie is going to bring him round to me at five o'clock.

1:00 p.m.
Mum's out and I am determined to make Robbie realise that I'm a great deal older than I was fifteen days ago. I haven't any money and Mum has selfishly taken her purse with her, but I HAVE A PLAN.

2:00 p.m.
There is some peroxide that Gran uses to clean her dentures when she comes to stay. It's kept in the bathroom cupboard and I'm going to use it to bleach a really sophisticated streak of blonde in my hair at the front.

2:30 p.m.
I've put it on, I wonder how long you have to leave it? It's stinging my scalp so that must be a good sign.

3:30 p.m.
It's gone a sort of orange colour! Oh bloody hell, I'll have to put some more on.

4:15 p.m.
Now it's gone sort of bright yellow. I look like a canary.

234

5:00 p.m.

Thank goodness it's gone white. I think it looks quite good. It feels a bit stiff, though. Oh well, it'll soften up in time. I think it makes me look at least four years older.

5:30 p.m.

Robbie here with Angus. I was so pleased to see him I tried to give him a cuddle but he lashed out at me and was hissing until I gave him a rabbit leg. Then he started purring. (Angus, not Robbie.)

Robbie noticed my hair when I stood up. He was obviously impressed because he said, "Er – you've got a white streak in your hair."

I said, "Oh yes, do you like it?"

There was a bit of a silence between us. I was thinking, Go on, kiss me, kiss me! But he said, "Look, this is not easy for me, I think I should go now."

I said, "Thank you for Angus."

He said, "Oh, that's OK, I knew you liked him and the scratches will heal in time and I should be able to replace the trousers."

As he was leaving I had one final go to make him see that

I was mature and sophisticated beyond my years. I flicked my hair back like they do in movies and then I made the mistake of running my fingers through my hair. The white streak snapped off in my hand. I was just left holding it there, in my hand. Robbie looked amazed. He looked at the hunk of hair in my hand and then he looked at me and then he started laughing. He said, "God you're weird," and then he kissed me. (I shoved the hunk of hair on the sofa and Angus pounced on it – he must have thought it was a hamster or something.)

After a bit of number six kissing Robbie said, "Well, look, let's take it easy and start seeing each other, shall we... see how it goes, maybe keep it a bit quiet from people at first?"

So all is well that ends well. I am now nearly Robbie's girlfriend, hahahaha. Summer love, summer love!!!

The end

9:00 p.m.
Mum came in. "Right, we're all set – I've got them!!"

I said (in a sort of romantic daze), "What have you got, Mutti?"

"I've got the tickets for us!"

"Tickets for what?"

"Tickets for New Zealand. When you said you wanted to go I went and booked them. Dad paid for them and we're off to Whangamata next week."

Sacré bloody *bleu* and *merde*!!!

Georgia's Glossary

airing cupboard · This is a cupboard over the top of the hot-water heater in a house. It is used for keeping towels and sheets warm on cold winter nights. Er, at least that's what it's used for in normal people's houses.

"Agadoo" · The worst song ever written. It won the Eurovision Song Contest, which is a competition for the worst songs ever written. That is all I have to say. Oh, and grown-ups think it is a "laugh" to sing it when they are drunk. It isn't. (It goes "Aga doo doo doo, Aga doo doo doo" for twenty hours.)

agony aunt · A woman in a magazine who gives you advice if you are a sad person with no one else to talk to. For instance, Jas might write, "Dear Agony Aunt, My friend Georgia is so much better-looking, cleverer and all-round more brilliant that I feel inadequate. What should I do?" And the agony aunt would write back, "Kill yourself." (Not really, that last bit is a joke.)

bangers · Firecrackers. Fireworks that just explode with a big bang. That's it. No pretty whooshing or stars or rocketing up into the sky. Bangers just bang. Boy fireworks. Boys are truly weird.

Borstal · A sort of young person's prison for naughty boys.

catsuit · An all-in-one suit thing with trousers and a zipper up the front. Usually evening wear. It is supposed to be sexy, and perhaps it is, but try getting out of one quickly if you have to pay an emergency lavatory call. Like a grown-up version of a romper suit.

Crazy Colour · Hair colour that you paint on your hair and that can be washed out.(Crazy because it is blue or purple or red or green.)

deely bopper · Like antenna things with tiny balls on the end that you wear on your head. Popular with five-year-olds.

Denise Van Outen · She is a blonde on TV who is a bit on the breasty side. Boys seem to like her, although I can't see the attraction myself as I am not (probably) a lesbian.

dole · What unemployed people get (i.e. money) to stop them starving to death. Welfare.

double cool with knobs · "Double" and "with knobs" are instead of saying "very" or "very, very, very, very". You'd feel silly saying, "He was very, very, very, very, very cool." Also everyone would fall asleep before you finished your sentence. So "double cool with knobs" is altogether snappier.

duffing up · Duffing up is the female equivalent of beating up. It is not so violent and usually involves a lot of pushing, with the occasional pinch.

first former · Kids of about eleven who have just started "big" school. They have shiny innocent faces – very tempting to slap.

fringe · Goofy short bit of hair that comes down to your eyebrows. Some one told me that American-type people call them "bangs", but this is so ridiculously strange that it's not worth thinking about. Some people can look very stylish with a fringe (i.e. me) while others look goofy (Jas). The Beatles started it (apparently). One of them had a German girlfriend and she cut their hair with a pudding bowl, and the rest is history.

Froggie and geoggers · Froggie is short for French; geoggers is short for geography. Ditto blodge (biology) and lunck (lunch).

full-frontal snogging · Kissing with all the trimmings: lip to lip, open mouth, tongues... everything. (Apart from dribble, which is never acceptable.)

gorgey · Gorgeous. Like fabby (fabulous) and marvy (marvellous).

"have the painters in" · An expression to indicate that a girl is... er... having her... you know what. Oh, come on, you do know. Having her... er... well, to put it plainly... her... well, that "the red flag is flying", that her "little friend has come to visit". Period. Menstruation. Woman trouble. Trouble at the mill. I can't go on with this; it is making me tired.

hols · Vacation. In olden days when bishops wanted a day off, they decided to have a Holy Day or, as it has become, a Hol-i-day. Shortened to hols for obvious reasons. (Life is too short to use long words.) Apart from the fact that Anne Boleyn, Henry VIII's wife, designed dresses with long sleeves because she had a sixth finger growing out of her little finger, this is the only thing I remember from history class.

"how's your father" · A boy's... er... penis (or penid as I thought it was until I was eleven). Well, you wanted to know.

jimjams · Pyjamas. Also pygmies or jammies.

joggerbums · Trousers that you jog in. Jogging trousers.

jumping-jacks · A hellish combination. This is about ten bangers all tied together. When a jumping-jack is lit, not only does it bang A LOT, but it leaps all over the place and chases you about. Banging. Boys think it is hilarious to light them and chuck them into a group of girls. As I have said, boys are weird.

naff · unbearably and embarrassingly out of fashion and nerdy. Naff things are: parents dancing to "modern" music, blue eyeshadow, blokes who wear socks with sandals, pigtails... You know what I mean.

nuddy-pants · Quite literally nude-coloured pants. And you know what nude-coloured pants are? They are no pants. So if you are in your nuddy-pants you are in your no pants (i.e. you are naked).

o-levels · "Ordinary" level exams that perfectly nice teenagers were made to take when they were about fifteen. Now called GCSEs. These exams are of course sadistically timed for the summer months by teachers, etc., who have no life and therefore want to spoil it for everyone else.

one-four-one · The code you dial before a number if you don't want the person you are calling to be able to trace your number. Like a secrecy code.

Paloma · Paloma is a perfume made up by Paloma Picasso, who is the daughter of the famous artist Picasso. Her dad used to paint people with eyes on their cheeks – he invented this. It is not bad art, apparently, but "abstract". Anyone could say that about anything that was really crap. They could say, "No, you are mistaken, this is not a really bad drawing of a cow that looks more like a monkey, it is abstract art." But perhaps I am cynical.

po-faced · a po is a sort of basin thing that goes under your bed, like a bedpan. In the old days very poor people would use a po instead of a lavatory. Then they poured the contents of the po out on to the streets on to innocent passersby. Ergo, "po-faced" means someone who has a face like a lavatory bowl.

poxy · From Olde Englishe. "The pox" was crumbly horrible spots that Olde Englishe people got from not having proper lavatories. Or maybe it was rats. I can't remember. Anyway, hence the expression "poxy", meaning horrible.

prat · A gormless oik. You make a prat of yourself by mistakenly putting both legs down one knicker leg or by playing air guitar at pop concerts.

PVC jacket · PVC is that shiny wet-look material that whatshername in *The Avengers* used to wear about a million years ago. PVC has come back into fashion again, but some things never will. Culottes, for instance, will never be fashionable again; they never were, apart from with Swiss people. I rest my case fashionwise.

Reeves and Mortimer · Reeves and Mortimer are a comedy double act. They are very mad indeed. But I like them.

romper-suit · All-in-one garment that some sadist designed for children. The legs and body and arms are all joined together, which makes it impossible to get on or off. (And in Libby's case, if she has an accidental poo attack in one, you can imagine the result.)

runner · An escape. Hence the saying, "to do a runner". To run away.

sandwich spread · Stuff in a jar that looks like throw-up that you spread on bread.

shirty · Flustered and twitchy and coming on all pompous.

stroppy · Stroppy is a very useful expression and is the state between having a nervy b (nervous breakdown) and a tantrum. For instance, you would get stroppy or "throw a strop" if your mum did not let you borrow her Chanel handbag, for no reason other than she says you would lose it. You would not quite have a nervy b because it is after all just a handbag. However, you are perfectly entitled to get stroppy if you can't have what you want.

swiz · An unfair thing. Another girl gets a boy you like, that is a swiz. One of your friends gets to pierce her navel and your boring vati won't let you. This is an obvious double swiz.

tosser · A special kind of prat.

TTFN · Ta ta for now. Ta ta means "goodbye". I think this is a World War II expression like "Chocks away" and

"Luftwaffe at 5 o'clock", but so much of life is a mystery to me, I can't be absolutely sure on this one.

wally · See "prat". A wally additionally has no clothes sense.

wet · Drippy, useless, nervy. Lindsay.

whelk · A horrible shellfish thing that only the truly mad (like my granded, for instance) eat. They are unbelievably slimy and mucuslike.

p.s.

Turn the page for a peek at
my next book...

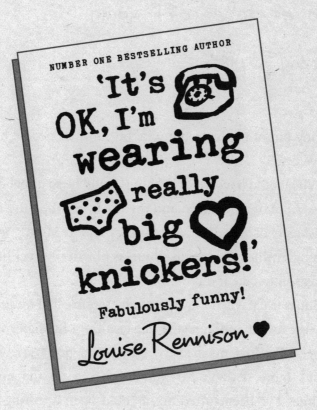

NUMBER ONE BESTSELLING AUTHOR

'It's OK, I'm wearing really big knickers!'

Fabulously funny!

Louise Rennison ♥

www.georgianicolson.com

The Sex God has landed...
and, er, taken off again

Sunday July 18th
My room
6:00 p.m.

Staring out of my bedroom window at other people having a nice life.

Who would have thought things could be so unbelievably pooey? I'm only fourteen and my life is over because of the selfishosity of so-called grown-ups. I said to Mum, "You are ruining my life. Just because yours is practically over there is no reason to take it out on me."

But as usual when I say something sensible and meaningful she just tutted and adjusted her bra like a Russian roulette player. (Or do I mean disco thrower? I don't know and, what's more, I don't care.) If I counted up the number of times I've been tutted at... I could open a tutting shop.

It's just SO not fair... How can my parents take me away from my mates and make me go to New Zealand? Who goes to New Zealand?

In the end, when I pointed out how utterly useless as a mum she was, she lost her rag and SHOUTED at me.

"Go to your room right now!"

I said, "All right, I'll go to my ROOM!! I WILL go to my room!! And do you know what I'll be doing in my room? No you don't, so I'll tell you! I'll be just BEING in my room. That's all. Because there is nothing else to do!!!!!!"

Then I just slammed off. Left her there. To think about what she has done.

Unfortunately it means that I am in my bed and it is only six o'clock.

7:00 p.m.

Oh Robbie, where are you now? Well, I know where you are now actually, but is this any time to go away on a footie trip?

On the bright side I am now the girlfriend of a Sex God.

7:15 p.m.

On the dark side, the Sex God doesn't know his new

girlfriend is going to be forced to go to the other (useless) side of the universe in a week's time.

7:18 p.m.
I can't believe that after all the time it has taken to trap the SG, all the make-up I have had to buy, the trailing about, popping up unexpectedly when he was out anywhere... all the planning... all the dreaming – it's gone to waste. I finally get him to snog me (number six) and he says, "Let's see each other but keep it quiet for a bit." And at that moment, with classic poo timing, Mutti says, "We're off to New Zealand next week."

My eyes are all swollen up like mice eyes from crying. Even my nose is swollen. It's not small at the best of times, but now it looks like I've got three cheeks. Marvellous. Thank you, God.

9:00 p.m.
I'll never get over this.

9:10 p.m.
Time goes very slowly when you are suicidal.

I put sunglasses on to hide my tiny mincers. They are new ones that Mum bought me in a pathetic attempt to interest me in going to Kiwi-a-gogo land. They looked quite cool, actually. I looked a bit like one of those French actresses who smoke Gauloise and cry a lot in between snogging Gerard Depardieu. I tried a husky French accent in the mirror.

"And zen when I was, how you say? *Une teen-ager, mes parents, mes très, très horriblement parents*, take me to *Nouvelle Zelande*. Ahh *merde!*"

At which point I heard Mum coming up the stairs and had to leap into bed. She popped her head round the door and said, "Georgie... are you asleep?"

I didn't say anything. That would teach her.

As she left she said, "I wouldn't sleep in the sunglasses if I were you, they might get embedded in your head."